Samuel French Acting Edition

Stand by Your Man
The Tammy Wynette Story

by Mark St. Germain

MUSIC USE NOTE

Licensees are solely responsible for obtaining formal written permission from copyright owners to use copyrighted music in the performance of this play and are strongly cautioned to do so. If no such permission is obtained by the licensee, then the licensee must use only original music that the licensee owns and controls. Licensees are solely responsible and liable for all music clearances and shall indemnify the copyright owners of the play(s) and their licensing agent, Samuel French, against any costs, expenses, losses and liabilities arising from the use of music by licensees. Please contact the appropriate music licensing authority in your territory for the rights to any incidental music.

IMPORTANT BILLING AND CREDIT REQUIREMENTS

If you have obtained performance rights to this title, please refer to your licensing agreement for important billing and credit requirements.

Stand By Your Man: The Tammy Wynette Story

Produced by
Gaylord Entertainment   Carolyn Rossi Copeland

Nicolette Hart
as
Tammy Wynette

with

Brad Albin, Miles Aubrey, Galen Butler, Terry Mike Jeffrey, Jenny Littleton,
David Lutken, Susan Mansur, Kevin Owens, Tricia Paoluccio, J. Robert Spencer

and

Jim Lauderdale
as
George Jones

Musical Arrangements	*Musical Director*	*Casting*	*Production Stage Manager*
Galen Butler	David Lutken	Dave Clemmons	Julie A. Richardson
Scenic Designer	*Lighting Designer*	*Costume Designer*	*Sound Designer*
Dennis C. Maulden	Todd O. Wren	Bridget R. Bartlett	Andrew Keister

Book by
Mark St. Germain

Directed and Staged by
Gabriel Barre

Project Conceived by Steve Buchanan

CAST OF CHARACTERS

Tammy Wynette

George Jones

MeeMaw

George Richey

Young Tammy

Euple Byrd

Don Chapel

Billy Sherrill

Burt Reynolds

Michael Tomlin

Various Ensemble Roles
Played By All
Actors Except
Tammy.

MUSICAL NUMBERS

Act One

Stand By Your Man
   Tammy Wynette by Billy Sherrill & Tammy Wynette
Why Baby Why
   George Jones, Young Tammy by Darrell Edwards & George Jones
I Saw The Light
   Company by Hank Williams
My Man (Understands)
   Young Tammy by Billy Sherrill, Carmol Taylor &n Norro Wilson
Between 29 and Danger
   Tammy Wynette, Dolly Pardon, Aggie by Bobby Braddock & Hazel Smith
The Race Is On
   George Jones by Don Rollins
Bedtime Story
   Tammy Wynette by Billy Sherrill & Glen Sutton
Apartment #9
   Tammy Wynette, Studio Singer by Johnny Paycheck, F. Foley, C. Owen
Your Good Girl's Gonna Go Bad
   Tammy Wynette, Studio Singer by Billy Sherrill & Glen Sutton
Love Bug
   George Jones by Curtis Wayne & Wayne Kemp
My Elusive Dreams
   Tammy Wynette, Georhe Jones by Bobby Braddock
D-I-V-O-R-C-E
   Tammy Wynette, George Jones by Bobby Braddock & Curly Putnam
(We're Not) The Jet Set
   Tammy Wynette, George Jones by Bobby Braddock
Near You
   Tammy Wynette, George Jones by Francis Craig & Kermit Goel
We're Gonna Hold On
   Tammy Wynette, George Jones by George Jones & Earle Montgomery
I Still Believe In Fairytales
   Tammy Wynette by Glenn Martin

Intermission

MUSICAL NUMBERS

Act Two

Another Chance
   Tammy Wynette, Band by Robert Drawdy, Dennis Knutson & Jerry L. Taylor
'Til I Can Make It On My Own
   Tammy Wynette by George Richey, Bill Sherrill & Tammy Wynette
Did You Ever
   Tammy Wynette, Burt Reynolds by Bobby Braddock
Golden Ring
   Tammy Wynette, George Jones by Bobby Braddock & Rafe VanHoy
You And Me
   Tammy Wynette by George Richey & Billy Sherrill
If Drinking Don't Kill Me (Her Memory Will)
   George Jones by R. Beresford & H. Sanders
'Til I Get It Right
   Tammy Wynette by Red Lane & Larry Henley
God's Gonna Get Me For That
   MeeMaw by E.E. Collins
Justified And Ancient
   Tammy Wynette, The KLF by James Cauty, Ricky Lyte & W. Drummond
Dear Daughters
   Tammy Wynette by Tammy Wynette
Singin' My Song
   Tammy Wynette by Bill Sherrill, Tammy Wynette & Glen Sutton
How Great Thou Art
   Young Tammy, Band by Stuart K. Hine
Stand By Your Man (Reprise)
   Tammy Wynette by Billy Sherrill & Tammy Wynette

THANKS

Carolyn would like to thank Jeff Matisoff for staying with and caring for this musical from Flat Rock to the Ryman to Casa Manana and Goodspeed. Mark would also like to thank his son, Daniel St. Germain, for his great spirit and production assistance. Carolyn would like to thank Steve Buchanan for entrusting her with the development of this musical.

VERY SPECIAL THANKS

Mark St. Germain and Carolyn Rossi Copeland would like to thank Tammy's four fabulous daughters, Gwendolyn, Jacqueline, Tina Louise and Georgette for their encouragement and their generous spirit during the development of this musical.

ACT I

The Ryman Auditorium – April 9, 1998

(The action of the play takes place during a forty-year period of Tammy Wynette's life. There is a single unit set with the band onstage in view of the audience at all times during the performance. There are scenic elements that provide suggestions of time and location. Except for the actor playing TAMMY, all other actor's/musicians play the numerous people who were a part of Tammy's Wynette's life, both living and deceased.
In darkness, the ANNOUNCER is heard.)

ANNOUNCER. Ladies and Gentlemen, the First Lady of Country Music, Miss Tammy Wynette.

(Lights up on Tammy's Band; TAMMY enters to applause.)

Song: *Stand By Your Man*

TAMMY.
STAND BY YOUR MAN
AND SHOW THE WORLD YOU LOVE HIM
KEEP GIVIN' ALL THE LOVE YOU CAN
STAND BY YOUR MAN

(A band member "Drops Out" musically. TAMMY, surprised, keeps singing. A second band member, then a third, drop out as a confused TAMMY tries to continue.)

STAND BY YOUR MAN
AND SHOW THE WORLD YOU LOVE HIM
KEEP GIVIN' ALL THE LOVE –

*(TAMMY stops; sees she's alone on stage. REV. MURRAY overlaps
her last words. Lights up on REV. JAMES MURRAY, speaking
at Tammy's Memorial Service.)*

REV. MURRAY. 'This is a glorious time that we can remember Tammy.'

*(As TAMMY'S voice is heard from the rear of the auditorium, REV..
MURRAY freezes, lights dimming on him.)*

TAMMY. *(Confused)* Reverend Murray, hold on now; I don't understand.
MURRAY. She loved Nashville, but she has taken up residence at a different location.
TAMMY. What?
MURRAY. Tammy has found peace because she has gone to her True Home at last.
TAMMY. My true home? Why are you talking about me like I'm –

*(Lights up reveals YOUNGER TAMMY WYNETTE picking cotton,
moving and humming to GEORGE JONES on the radio, "Why
Baby Why", which continues throughout.)*

Itawambia County, Missippi – Outside The Pugh Cabin, 1959

Song: *Why Baby Why*

GEORGE JONES AND YOUNGER TAMMY.
TELL ME WHY BABY, WHY BABY, WHY BABY WHY
YOU MAKE ME CRY BABY, CRY BABY, CRY BABY, CRY

(TAMMY stares, taken aback.)

TAMMY. What in the world…?

GEORGE JONES AND YOUNGER TAMMY.
LORD, I CAN'T HELP BUT LOVE YOU 'TIL THE DAY I DIE
SO TELL ME, WHY BABY, WHY BABY, WHY BABY WHY…

*(Lights up on MEEMAW, TAMMY'S mother, calling out to young
TAMMY from their cabin. MEEMAW wears thick black glasses.)*

MEEMAW. Virginia Wynette Pugh, you better pick more and
sing less, do you hear me?
TAMMY. MeeMaw. It can't be you!
YOUNGER TAMMY. Yes, Ma'am.
TAMMY. And that's me! I can't believe it! And don't I look
good.

(MEEMAW turns to face TAMMY.)

MEEMAW. 'Course you do; you're my daughter. Who do you
think you got it from?
TAMMY. But MeeMaw! You're dead!
MEEMAW. Thank you for the news. Don't you think I know
it? That's why I'm up here with you and not out there with them!

(MEEMAW points toward the AUDIENCE.)

TAMMY. I don't understand-
MEEMAW. Just hush and listen. *(To Band, cutting them off.)*
I said, Hush! You see, when most people pass on from there to here
they watch their whole lives flash before their eyes in one single
blink. But not you. With a house full of kids, five husbands, and
the fact you never met a song you didn't like, you'd be blinking up
a Twister. So that's why I'm here; to help you see your way true and
clear.

GEORGE AND YOUNGER TAMMY.
LORD I CAN'T HELP BUT LOVE YOU 'TIL THE DAY I DIE
SO TELL ME WHY, BABY, WHY BABY, WHY BABY WHY

TAMMY. Where are we?
MEEMAW. Itawamba County, Mississippi. *(Points)* There's
our cabin your Granddaddy built with his own hands.

TAMMY. George Jones is on the radio.

MEEMAW. And there you are, picking cotton and pretending you're on stage right next to him. *(Calls to YOUNGER TAMMY.)* Girl, you fill that sack full! And turn off that radio!

YOUNGER TAMMY. Yes, Ma'am.

TAMMY. *(Proud)* I could pick 204 pounds a day.

MEEMAW. Even more if... you stuffed your sack with rocks and set the Cotton Gin on fire.

TAMMY. MeeMaw, I did that once!

MEEMAW. Because you got a good whipping. And the Good Lord knows you deserved it!

The Church In Itawamba County

(Music changes from Why Baby Why, to church music. TAMMY puts down her bag, readies herself for church. She moves into a stained glass light.)

TAMMY. That's our Church!

MEEMAW. I don't know what they liked better: Praying or Playing.

PREACHER. AMEN!

YOUNG TAMMY. *(Freely, ad-lib.)* Praise the Lord!

TAMMY. *(To MEEMAW.)* And once I learned how to play Daddy's old guitar, then we really got cookin'.

Song: *I Saw The Light*

YOUNG TAMMY.
I WANDERED SO AIMLESS
MY LIFE FILLED WITH SIN
I WOULDN'T LET MY
DEAR SAVIOR IN

YOUNG TAMMY & MEEMAW.
THEN JESUS CAME LIKE
A STRANGER IN THE NIGHT

ALL.
PRAISE THE LORD-

I SAW THE LIGHT
I SAW THE LIGHT
I SAW THE LIGHT
NO MORE DARKNESS
NO MORE NIGHT
NOW I'M SO HAPPY
NO SORROW IN SIGHT
PRAISE THE LORD
I SAW THE LIGHT

(The handsome EUPLE BYRD enters the church.)

 EUPLE.
I WAS A FOOL TO
WANDER AND STRAY

 PREACHER. Sing it brother Euple!

 EUPLE. (CONT.)
STRAIGHT IS THE GATE
AND NARROW THE WAY
NOW I HAVE TRADED
THE WRONG FOR THE RIGHT;
PRAISE THE LORD
I SAW THE LIGHT

 COMPANY.
I SAW THE LIGHT
I SAW THE LIGHT
NO MORE DARKNESS
NO MORE NIGHT

(EUPLE and YOUNG TAMMY'S eyes make contact.)

NOW I'M SO HAPPY
NO SORROW IN SIGHT
PRAISE THE LORD

 YOUNG TAMMY. *(Looks at EUPLE, then heavenward.)*
Thank you, Jesus!

I SAY THE LIGHT

(Church disperses leaving YOUNG TAMMY with EUPLE. MEEMAW & TAMMY watch from a distance.)

EUPLE. Hey.
YOUNG TAMMY. Hey.
TAMMY. Oh no.
EUPLE. I don't know if you remember me. You went to school with by Brother, D.C. I'm Euple Byrd. And you are-
MEEMAW. Hooked like a fish.
TAMMY. *(To MeeMaw.)* Stop her!
MEEMAW. Don't you think I tried?
YOUNG TAMMY. My friends call me Wynette.
EUPLE. What are you doing after Church?
MEEMAW. Going straight to hell.
YOUNG TAMMY. *(To EUPLE.)* Let's go!
MEEMAW. Wynette! He's too old for you! He's been in the army! That boy knows things you shouldn't even guess at.
YOUNG TAMMY. MeeMaw!
MEEMAW. The answer is "no"!
YOUNG TAMMY. That's always your answer! And I'm ready for "yes"!
MEEMAW. *(To TAMMY.)* You try talking to you!

(MUSIC intro begins, YOUNG TAMMY pulls away.)

Song: My Man (Understands)

YOUNG TAMMY.
MY MAN UNDERSTANDS
HE HOLDS ME IN THE PALM OF HIS HAND
AND I LIKE IT, I LIKE IT
HE'S A DREAM, THE REAL THING
HE ALWAYS MAKES ME FEEL LIKE A QUEEN
AND I LOVE IT, I LOVE IT

HIS ARMS, ARE WARM
THEY KEEP ME AWAY FROM HARM

AND I'M PROUD OF IT, SO PROUD OF IT
HE'S MINE, HE'S FINE
HE MAKES A FUNNY FEELING GO UP MY SPINE
AND I WANT TO KEEP IT LIKE THIS ALL THE TIME

HE'S GOT WHAT I WANT, WHEN I WANT IT
HE'S GOT WHAT I NEED, WHEN I NEED IT
I'D FIND A MILLION JUST TO KEEP IT
JUST TO KEEP ON HOLDING TO THE PRECIOUS LOVE HE
GIVES ME

MY MAN UNDERSTANDS
HE HOLDS ME IN THE PALM OF HIS HAND
AND I WANT TO KEEP IT LIKE THIS
ALL THE TIME

EUPLE. *(Pulling TAMMY close.)* I want you to marry me.

YOUNG TAMMY. They'd throw me out of high school. Graduation's only a few months away.

EUPLE. I can't wait that long.

(MEE MAW steps into the light, eyeing TAMMY and EUPLE.)

MEEMAW. You're late! Thirty Minutes! You've got no respect for her or me! *(To YOUNG TAMMY)* And you're not seeing him again.

YOUNG TAMMY. Oh yes I am.

MEEMAW. Oh no you're not.

YOUNG TAMMY. Well, if I can't see him, then I'll marry him!

MEEMAW. That's the stupidest thing I've ever heard. If you're that dumb...

TAMMY. *(Watching them argue.)* Don't say it.

MEEMAW. ...go ahead and marry him.

YOUNG TAMMY. Okay I will!

MEEMAW. Wynette, think with your head! Do you remember your Daddy?

BOTH TAMMY AND YOUNG TAMMY. *(Defensive)* Sure I do.

MEEMAW. But you don't. You were nine months old when he died. You remember because you want to believe you do. Like now. You want to believe some man like Euple Byrd can take your Daddy's place. But he can't. No man can…

YOUNG TAMMY. Meemaw, don't say that. All that leaves me is alone.

Song: My Man (Understands) Reprise

YOUNG TAMMY.
HE'S GOT WHAT I WANT WHEN I WANT IT
HE'S GOT WHAT I NEED WHEN I NEED IT
I'D FIGHT A MILLION JUST TO KEEP IT
JUST TO KEEP ON HOLDING TO THE PRECIOUS
LOVE HE GIVES ME

MY MAN, UNDERSTANDS
HE HOLDS ME IN THE PALM OF HIS HAND
AND I WANT TO KEEP IT LIKE THIS ALL THE TIME

JUSTICE. You may kiss the bride. *(YOUNG TAMMY & EUPLE lock lips.)* That'll do.

TAMMY.
AND I WANT TO KEEP IT LIKE THIS ALL THE TIME

(As PREACHER exits an old beds rolls out. TAMMY and EUPLE are alone.)

The Euple Family Home

YOUNG TAMMY. Gosh. That was so fast I barely got in my "I Do".

EUPLE. It's fine by me. Gives us more time for *(He pushes on bed springs, which squeak loudly)* our Honeymoon Night. *(TAMMY looks warily at the BED; EUPLE strides toward her, machismo on two legs, then past her, calling offstage.)* 'Night Momma, Pop, D.C., Darlene, Rita Fay. Sparky.

(ALL the family members respond when there name is called, even the dog, ala "The Waltons" this is done ad lib by the band members who are huddled up stage center outside an imaginary door.)

YOUNG TAMMY. Euple; this just doesn't seem, well, private.

EUPLE. Of course it's private! It's my room! *(EUPLE sits on the bed, the springs shriek loudly. As he bounces up and down they shriek even louder. The sound of the bed is done on an electric guitar.)* Hop on!

(TAMMY, gently, climbs in, but the springs shreik again.)

YOUNG TAMMY. Aren't these springs kind of loud?

EUPLE. Nobody's listening. *(Offstage sound of parents, sisters and brothers snorting with laughter.)* Mrs. Byrd; you scoot right over here.

(Springs shriek again, YOUNG TAMMY jumps up.)

YOUNG TAMMY. Maybe we should sleep on the floor.

EUPLE. Sugar, I've got a surprise for you, a big one.

YOUNG TAMMY. All right, I'm ready.

EUPLE. You and me are going to do some traveling.

YOUNG TAMMY. *(Excited)* Really?

EUPLE. You betcha. I lost my job.

(Lights go down and the sound of springs is replaced by a baby's cry. MEEMAW enter carrying baby, give it to YOUNG TAMMY. YOUNG TAMMY steps into light carrying a swaddled infant. EUPLE joins her.)

YOUNG TAMMY. Gwendolyn Lee Byrd. Isn't she the most beautiful baby ever born?

EUPLE. She sure is. And her daddy just got a new job in Tupelo!

(MEEMAW appears in the light beside them, holding her bunched apron apron. Neither TAMMY nor EUPLE hear her.)

MEEMAW. *(To the audience.)* Where he got laid off again.

(TAMMY registers this disappointment, EUPLE takes his bundled baby, whispering to it.)

EUPLE. But don't you worry, little one. Because Daddy found himself a job in Red Bay.
MEEMAW. Lost that one, too.

(Sound of baby crying, TAMMY [Older] Enters carrying another baby from upstage and in a turn around replaces YOUNG TAMMY. YOUNG TAMMY give TAMMY the first baby.)

TAMMY. *(Holding both babies.)* Now Gwen's got a sister! "Jackie"; just like Mrs. Kennedy.

Log Cabin On Pugh Property

EUPLE. *(Gestures toward 'building" before him.)* And we got our own White House; the Byrds are living in style.
MEEMAW. *(To audience.)* A log shack, on its best day. And on my property. Sorry, honey, but you asked for it. You're a grown up now.

(MEE MAW exits. Both Babies Begin to cry. TAMMY sings to quiet them.)

TAMMY.
HUSH LITTLE BABIES DON'T YOU CRY
MAMA'S GONNA SING YOU A LULLABY-

EUPLE. Maybe that's why she's crying.
TAMMY. Euple!
EUPLE. Well, maybe they don't like Hillbilly Music. My family doesn't. They see your guitar come in the front door they run out the back.
TAMMY. *(Indignant)* I don't care what they do. I like to sing.
EUPLE. You've got plenty of time to sing here, don't you? Alone? You can sing when you're walking to the spring for water or

boiling diapers in the fireplace

TAMMY. Euple, that's not what I'm talking about. It's just that I want to be doing, well, something more with my life.

EUPLE. More?

TAMMY. It sounds crazy. But don't laugh. *(Pause)* I want to go to Beauty School.

EUPLE. Come on, Sugar; you don't look that bad after two kids.

TAMMY. Beautician's School! I want to get my license; I want to work. *(No reaction; EUPLE stares.)* Euple? What do you think?

EUPLE. You know; that might not be as stupid as it sounds.

TAMMY. Really?

EUPLE. I just got a job at Taylor Construction. That means going on the road; two, maybe three weeks at a shot. *(Hands GWEN back to TAMMY, who now holds two.)* You might as well be doing something while I'm gone.

American Beauty Academy

(EUPLE exits. Lights up on DOLLY PARDON, owner of the American Beauty Academy and AGGIE one of her clients, to whom she is giving a perm. The actress has on a wig that is set with roller for except four that DOLLY and TAMMY put on.)

DOLLY PARDON. I went right back at her. I said, "Flora Dell, you've got a wooden leg. What do you care where his hand was?"

(TAMMY enters, nervous.)

TAMMY. Excuse me, is this the American Beauty College?

DOLLY. *(Stops, fluffs her hair.)* Can't you tell?

TAMMY. Well, I'd be very interested to apply if I could pay week by week, on account that I've got babysitting to pay for, too. *(Realizes she hasn't introduced herself.)* I'm sorry; I'm Virginia Wynette Byrd. My friends call me "Wynette".

DOLLY. Wynette, I'm Dolly Pardon. *(They shake hands.)*

(AGGIE lowers the magazine she has been reading.)

AGGIE. That's – P-A-R-D-O-N. It's what they call "ironic". *(Raises magazine again.)*

DOLLY. *(To TAMMY.)* You know, Beauty Care is not just a scientific or artistic skill. It takes a personal touch as well. People who get into this chair don't just want to look good; they want to feel good about themselves. So a Beauty Care Professional has to learn when to talk and when to listen. Because nothing brings out a woman's deepest emotions like a good rinse and a permanent. *(Motions for TAMMY to take over combing and cutting.)* Now why don't you jump right in here.

(Music begins.)

TAMMY. But what if I can't think of anything to say?
DOLLY. Then honey, you would be the first.

Song: *Between Twenty-Nine And Danger*

TAMMY.
I MADE UP MY MIND TODAY WHILE MAKING UP MY BED
THAT I'D MAKE UP MY FACE INSTEAD OF BAKING UP SOME
    BREAD

DOLLY. That's right!
AGGIE. Sing it, girl!

TAMMY.
TIRED OF PUTTING UP WITH SOMEONE WHO PUTS ME
    DOWN
SO I PUT ON MY BRAND NEW DRESS AND I SNEAKED OFF
    TO TOWN

ALL.
BETWEEN TWENTY-NINE AND DANGER
IN THE ARMS OF A STRANGER
BUT THAT KIND OF DANGER WOULD BE SWEET
WOULD BE SWEET RELIEF TO ME

TAMMY.
WHILE HE TOOK A BATH I GRABBED HIS CAR KEYS FROM

THE SHELF
THEN I WENT THROUGH HIS BILLFOLD AND FOR ONCE I
    HELPED MYSELF
I'VE WASHED SOCKS AND SHIRTS AND SHORTS AND
    DISHES FOR THAT MAN
BUT TODAY THE ONLY THING I'M WASHING IS MY HAND

ALL.
BETWEEN TWENTY NINE AND DANGER
IN THE ARMS OF A STRANGER
BUT THAT KIND OF DANGER WOULD BE SWEET
WOULD BE SWEET RELIEF TO ME

<u>Log Cabin On Pugh Property</u>

(Lights up on EUPLE embracing TAMMY.)

EUPLE. The kids are asleep.

TAMMY. No, Euple.

EUPLE. Why not? You've got nothing to worry about but fixing hair and babies and you're still crankier than a cat under water.

TAMMY. I told you, I've got a Kidney infection. The Doctor says-

EUPLE. Forget him! *(Hugs her again.)* What you need's a dose of Doc Euple's Love Medicine.

TAMMY. Euple, please. I feel sick and sad *(Pulls away.)* and I don't want that right now.

EUPLE. *(Annoyed)* Maybe we'd better talk to the Doctor about fixing that, too.

(Lights down on EUPLE, TAMMY crosses downstage.)

TAMMY.
I'M NOT OLD I'M LIKE MY CAR
I'VE GOT SOME GOOD YEARS LEFT
BUT THE THOUGHT OF GROWING OLD WITH HIM
    SCARES ME TO DEATH
GOT TO LEARN TO WALK ALONE BEFORE HE
    MAKES ME CRAWL

I'D RATHER BE A COMMON TRAMP THEN NOTHING AT
 ALL

 ALL.
BETWEEN TWENTY NINE AND DANGER
IN THE ARMS OF A STRANGER
BUT THAT KIND OF DANGER WOULD BE SWEET
WOULD BE SWEET RELIEF TO ME

<u>Doctor's Office</u>

*(Lights up on Doctor's Office, TAMMY and EUPLE. The Doctor
 places a bottle of pills on the desk. Speaking directly to
 EUPLE.)*

DOCTOR.. Mr. Byrd; we've had some success with a combination of medication and the Electroshock treatments. But, under the circumstances, I can't recommend any more.
 EUPLE. *(To TAMMY.)* Do you feel better?
 TAMMY. I feel… different. I don't cry so much. The pills help.

(She takes the bottle of pills and puts them in her pocket.)

 EUPLE. *(Pleased)* You see that! I knew it! Now you've got your head on straight.
 TAMMY. Euple, I want a divorce.
 EUPLE. You what?
 DOCTOR. *(Pause)* Mr. Byrd-
 EUPLE. Get your things. I'll wait in the car. *(Exits)*
 DOCTOR. *(To TAMMY.)* Mrs. Byrd, you've got to tell him that you're pregnant.
 TAMMY. I can't. And, please, don't you be telling him, either.

*(Lights out on Doctor's Office; TAMMY crosses stage. Lights up on
 American Beauty Academy. TAMMY enters light.)*

<u>American Beauty Academy - 1963</u>

*(TAMMY and DOLLY put the finishing touches on AGGIE'S hair: it
 looks terrible – a frizzy "bad perm" wig.)*

Song: *Twenty-Nine And Danger (Cont.)*

TAMMY, DOLLY AND AGGIE.
BETWEEN TWENTY-NINE AND DANGER
IN THE ARMS OF A STRANGER
BUT THAT KIND OF DANGER WOULD BE SWEET
WOULD BE SWEET RELIEF TO ME

(At end of chorus AGGIE lowers magazine to reveal new "look".)

DOLLY. You look so much younger!
AGGIE. I do?
DOLLY. You do.
AGGIE. Girl, you've got some voice in that throat of yours.
That's a gift from God.

(AGGIE tips TAMMY. DOLLY stares at her hair as AGGIE exits.)

DOLLY. Oh Lord, yes. That's the "Struck By Lighting"
Bouffant.

(TAMMY is suddenly frozen, one hand on her belly.)

TAMMY. Oh no. Dolly, this can't be.
DOLLY. Aggie's not much of a tipper.
TAMMY. Dolly! My water broke!
DOLLY. You're not six months yet-
TAMMY. Well, this baby can't count.

*(Sound of a Storm and Music: "Between Twenty Nine And Danger"
underscores as DOLLY puts TAMMY in a Wheel-Chair, push-
ing her across the stage to the hospital.)*

<u>Hospital</u>

NURSE. *(Blocking entrance.)* Insurance?
TAMMY. I don't have any.
NURSE. Cash?
TAMMY. I don't have much with me.

NURSE. Well, I'm sorry-

DOLLY. You will be. Because my friend is not going to have her baby in your Lobby! So move your sorry self or get ready to kiss some linoleum.

(DOLLY pushes TAMMY past the NURSE; The NURSE jumps out of her way, calling after them.)

NURSE. Don't you hot rod in this hospital!

(Song begins at top of this transition,. Once TAMMY is set lights up on TAMMY is a hospital bed, she hold a transistor radio. A song is playing, it is GEORGE JONE: The Race Is On, TAMMY weak, sings along quietly.)

Song: <u>_The Race Is On_</u>

GEORGE JONES.
AND THE RACE IS ON AND HERE COMES PRIDE UP THE
    BACKSTRETCH
HEARTACHES ARE GOIN' TO THE INSIDE
MY TEARS ARE HOLDIN' BACK
THEY'RE TRYING NOT TO FALL
MY HEART'S OUT OF THE RUNNIN'
TRUE LOVES SCRATCHED FOR ANOTHER SAVE
AND THE RACE IS ON AND IT LOOKS LIKE HEARTACHES
AND THE WINNER LOSES ALL

ONE DAY I VENTURED IN LOVE
NEVER ONCE SUSPECTIN' WHAT THE
FINAL RESULT WOULD BE
HOW I LIVED IN FEAR
WAKIN' UP EACH MORNIN'
AND FINDIN' THAT YOU'D
GONE FROM ME

(DOLLY PARDON enters to visit. TAMMY embraces her and she turns off the radio.)

WELL THIS ACHIN' AND PAIN IN MY HEART
FOR THIS DAY, IT WAS THE ONE I HATED TO FACE
SOMEBODY NEW CAME TO WIN HER
AND I CAME UP IN SECOND PLACE

DOLLY. I just saw her, down the hall. She's a cutie.

TAMMY. Two pounds, three ounces. The Doctor says she'll have to stay in that incubator 'till she gets stronger.

DOLLY. Well, she will. Because she's a fighter like her Mama.

TAMMY. Tina Denise. The Nurse calls her "Tiny".

(TAMMY and DOLLY smile.)

DOLLY. Tina suits her. Now you've got yourself three little Princesses. *(Takes out an envelope.)* Here's something for their Queen.

(TAMMY opens it, she is thrilled.)

TAMMY. My Diploma! Dolly! But I didn't finish half my courses. I'll come back-

DOLLY. *(Quickly)* No, no. That's all right. But tell me something, honey: what do you want to do now?

TAMMY. Well, I don't know. I wanted my diploma. This was my dream.

DOLLY. Is this what you'd really love to do all your life: work in a Beauty Parlor? And I mean "love"; love as much as you love those girls of yours?

TAMMY. Well; I love to sing. But so does everybody. I've got a family to support. How would I ever do that?

DOLLY. Sounds to me you've got to dream bigger.

(Lights down on DOLLY and TAMMY, up on MEEMAW.)

Log Cabin On Pugh Property

(TAMMY is packing, her suitcase.)

MEEMAW. Nashville!?

TAMMY. That's right. And I'm divorcing Euple.

MEEMAW. And disgracing this family.

TAMMY. I expected you to say that. What I didn't expect is you siding with Euple. Taking my children from me. Making me fight to get them back.

MEEMAW. I did what needed to be done.

TAMMY. They are my Children!

MEEMAW. They're my Grandchildren. And they're not going to spend their childhood plunked in a hot parking lot waiting for their Mother to get another door slammed in her face. Wake up, Girl! You never won a single Talent Contest you ever entered! I told you to learn Baton Twirling, but you never listened to me! Well, you'd better start now. Because nobody in Nashville's going to hire you unless they're looking for a full-time failure.

TAMMY. I might fail as a singer but I will not fail as a mother. My children are coming with me and I won't let you or Euple to get in our way.

(Takes guitar.)

MEEMAW. What do you think you're doing?

TAMMY. Taking Daddy's Guitar; I played it all my life.

MEEMAW. You're just like him, you know that? Your head in the clouds, always thinking what you want, always one foot out the door!

TAMMY. Not this time, MeeMaw. I've got two-

(TAMMY turns. EUPLE has entered blocking her way. TAMMY steps toward him. MEEMAW exits.)

EUPLE. You really think you're going to be one of those Hillbilly singers?

TAMMY. Yes I do.

EUPLE. Dream on, Baby. Dream on. *(He exits.)*

(TAMMY leaves with suitcase, her diploma in her purse and her guitar.)

<u>Anchor Motel - Nashville</u>

(Lights up on the lobby of the Anchor Motel, Nashville. The desk clerk DON CHAPEL is behind the counter. Evening. TAMMY enters exhausted. DON is not aware that she has approached the desk, he is composing a song. TAMMY presses the desk bell.)

TAMMY. Hi; I need a room for myself, my two girls under five, and my baby. But if you add us up, we're just two and a half adults.

DON. Are you a Singer or a Songwriter?

TAMMY. *(Reaching her limit.)* Mister, in the last month I've lost a dozen rooms when I said I was either. And if I hear the word "Hillbilly" one more time I'll be over this counter before you can stick your nose up.

DON. My name's Don Chapel. I'm a singer-songwriter. I'm just working this motel 'til I break in. How long have you been in town?

TAMMY. Long enough to knock on every door.

DON. Well then, tomorrow you just have to start knocking all over again. *(Slides TAMMY the guest book.)* How many nights?

TAMMY. That depends on your rate.

DON. *(Giving TAMMY a break.)* Well, let's see. *(Looks at book.)* It looks like you qualify for both the Boy Scout and Clergy discounts, so that'll come to, oh, three dollars a night. How's that work for you?

TAMMY. That works out to two nights and two meals. Thank you, Don.

DON. You're welcome. Us Hillbilly's got to stick together.

(LIGHTS fade on Hotel desk as TAMMY crosses to center in a down light. The stage is dark except for her light.)

<u>Billy Sherrill's Office</u>

TAMMY. Hello? Is anybody-

BILLY SHERRILL. *(Lights come up dimly.)* Yeah?

TAMMY. I'm looking for Mister Billy Sherrill's Office.

BILLY SHERRILL. *(In darkness.)* Yeah.

TAMMY. The Billy Sherrill who writes and produces for Epic Records-

BILLY SHERRILL. *(Impatient)* You found him. Come in here.

(Lights up on BILLY SHERRILL, he has feet in cowboy boots on his desk, he is leaning back in his chair, he lights a cigarette, starring at TAMMY. His expression is stoic, unreadable throughout.)

TAMMY. I'm sorry, but there was no Secretary or Receptionist so I just-

BILLY SHERRILL. What do you want?

TAMMY. A recording contract.

BILLY SHERRILL. And everybody in hell wants ice water.

(TAMMY smiles, nervous. BILLY SHERRILL stares.)

BILLY SHERRILL. You have a tape?

TAMMY. No, but I'll sing for you. *(Waits for a response.)*

BILLY SHERRILL. So do it.

(TAMMY begins to play and sing doing a George Jones impression.)

TAMMY.
TELL ME WHY BABY, WHY BABY, WHY BABY WHY
YOU MAKE ME CRY BABY, CRY BABY, CRY BABY CRY

BILLY SHERRILL. *(Interrupting)* George Jones.

TAMMY. He's the best.

BILLY SHERRILL. He is. Now let me hear what you sound like.

(TAMMY sings excerpt of "How Great Thou Art")

TAMMY.
THEN SING S MY SOUL

MY SAVIOR GOD TO THEE
HOW GREAT THOU ART
HOW GREAT THOU ART

BILLY SHERRILL. *(Interrupts)* What's your name?
TAMMY. Virginia Wynette Bird. I'm dropping the Bird and going back to Pugh. But my friends call me Wynette.
BILLY SHERRILL. Live here?
TAMMY. Not yet, I'm staying at the Anchor Motel. I'm leaving tomorrow, but I can-
BILLY SHERRILL. I'll call you. *(SHERRILL puts his feet down, resumes the paperwork on his desk.)*
TAMMY. Thank you, Mr. Sherrill. Thank you for...

(Phone rings, he picks it up.)

BILLY SHERRILL. What? I told you not to call me at work. No. No. No. No. No. All right, stop your crying. Happy birthday, Momma.

Anchor Motel, Nashville

(Lights up on motel room. TAMMY enters, gently putting down her guitar. Her oldest, GWEN, is barley seen in the dark, wrapped up in a blanket on the bed. MEEMAW ENTERS looking on.)

GWEN. Mama? Did he like you?
TAMMY. That man wouldn't get excited if the Angel Gabriel dropped by to play Trumpet.
GWEN. I miss MeeMaw.
TAMMY. So do I. *(Pause)* Sometimes.
GWEN. Mama, tell me a story. Please?
TAMMY. Alright.

Song: *Bedtime Story*

TAMMY.
ONCE UPON A TIME THERE WAS A CASTLE
AND IN THIS CASTLE LIVED A KING AND QUEEN

AND IT CAME TO PASS THEY BOTH WERE BLESSED
BY ONE LITTLE BLUE EYED PRINCESS
WITH THE SOFTEST GOLDEN CURLS YOU'VE EVER SEEN

BUT THEN ONE DAY HE MET THIS PRETTY LADY
AND SHE HAD LOTS OF PRETTY WORDS TO SAY
AND THIS PART MAKES YOUR MOMMY SAD
'CAUSE OH WHAT BIG EYES SHE HAD
AND SHE TOOK HIS HAND AND LED HIM FAR AWAY

STILL IT'S JUST ANOTHER BEDTIME STORY
BUT TELLING IT BRINGS TEARDROPS TO MY EYES
JUST ANOTHER PRETTY BED TIME STORY
SO PLEASE FORGIVE MOMMY IF SHE CRIES
WON'T YOU PLEASE FORGIVE MOMMY IF SHE CRIES

(Sound: Knock on the door.)

TAMMY. Come in.

(TAMMY goes to the door. Lights up on DON CHAPEL.)

DON. Wynette? You got a call downstairs.
TAMMY. From who?
DON. Billy Sherrill. He asked if you want to make a record.
TAMMY. *(Stunned)* When?
DON. Tonight.
TAMMY. Oh Lord.
DON. Good luck. Hey, if he needs any songs-
TAMMY. Sure Don, thank you.

(DON hands her her sweater.)

<u>Recording Studio – Sound Booth</u>

(Lights down on the motel; Lights up on BILLY SHERRILL in his studio. The band's assembled for the recording session. TAMMY enters; She goes over to the microphone.)

TAMMY. Mr. Sherrill?

BILLY SHERRILL. I'm in here. *(Speaking from his band position into microphone.)*

TAMMY. I can't tell you what this means —

BILLY SHERRILL. Don't. This song was recorded by Bobby Austin on a small label that didn't get much play. I think if we release it on Epic it could be a hit. Blondie; you take the lead. Let's hear it.

TAMMY. *(Calling to him.)* Okay!

Song: *Apartment #9*

BOTH.
JUST FOLLOW THE STAIRWAY
TO THIS LONELY WORLD OF MINE
YOU'LL FIND ME WAITING HERE
IN APARTMENT NUMBER NINE

TAMMY.
NOT SO VERY LONG AGO
YOU WALKED AWAY FROM ME
AND AFTER ALL THE PLANS WE MADE
YOU DECIDED TO BE FREE

ALL.
LONELINESS SURROUNDS ME
WITHOUT YOUR ARMS AROUND ME
AND THE SUN WILL NEVER SHINE
IN APARTMENT NUMBER NINE
NO THE SUN WILL NEVER SHINE
IN APARTMENT NUMBER NINE

MUSICIAN ONE. *(To BILLY.)* She's the real deal!
MUSICIAN TWO. Who is she?
BILLY. I'm going to figure that right now.

(BILLY Approaches TAMMY.)

BILLY SHERRILL. You need a new name.

TAMMY. *(Taken aback.)* I do?

BILLY SHERRILL. You don't look like a Bird or a Pugh. They don't fit you.

TAMMY. What does?

BILLY SHERRILL. Blonde Hair, skinny: let's see. You look like a Tammy.

TAMMY. Can I keep the "Wynette"?

BILLY SHERRILL. You ever sing in front of a big audience?

TAMMY. No.

BILLY SHERRILL. You want some advice?

TAMMY. Sure.

BILLY SHERRILL. Don't blow it.

(BILLY exits band begins to play. TAMMY steps on a stage for the first time.)

TAMMY. *(Nervous)* Hello, everybody. It's a real honor to sing at your Hoof and Harness Stock Show and - *(She's passed her song cue, jumps in quickly.)*

Song: *Your Good Girl's Gonna Go Bad*

TAMMY.
I'VE NEVER SEEN THE INSIDE OF A BAR ROOM
OR LISTENED TO A JUKEBOX ALL NIGHT LONG
BUT I SEE THESE ARE THE THINGS THAT GIVE YOU PLEA-
SURE
SO I'M GONNA MAKE SOME CHANGES IN OUR HOME

I'VE HEARD IT SAID IF YOU CAN'T BEAT 'EM, JOIN 'EM
SO IF THAT'S THE WAY YOU WANTED ME TO BE
I'LL CHANGE IF IT TAKES THAT TO MAKE YOU HAPPY
FROM NOW ON YOU'RE GONNA SEE A DIFFERENT ME

BECAUSE YOUR GOOD GIRL'S A-GONNA GO BAD
I'M GONNA BE THE SWINGIN'EST SWINGER YOU'VE
EVER HAD
IF YOU LIKE 'EM PAINTED UP, POWDERED UP
THEN YOU OUGHTA BE GLAD

'CAUSE YOUR GOOD GIRL'S A-GONNA GO BAD

TAMMY. Oh, no thank you sir, I dont's chew.

I'VE EVEN LEARNED TO LIKE THE TASTE OF WHSKEY
IN FACT YOU'LL HARDLY RECOGNIZE YOUR WIFE
I'LL BUY SOME BRAND NEW CLOTHES AND DRESS UP
FANCY
FOR MY JOURNEY TO THE WILDER SIDE OF LIFE
BECAUSE YOUR GOOD GIRL'S A-GONNA GO BAD
I'M GONNA BE THE SWINGIN'EST SWINGER YOU EVER
HAD
IF YOU LIKE 'EM PAINTED UP POWDERED UP
THEN YOU OUGHTA BE GLAD

'CAUSE YOUR GOOD GIRL'S A-GONNA GO BAD
OH YEAH YOUR GOOD GIRL'S A GONNA GO BAD

*(Light's change; Sound of telephone ringing. Lights up to reveal
MEEMAW picking up the telephone. MEEMAW has a glass of
lemonade in her hand.)*

<u>Winnipeg – Backstage On Tour - 1967</u>

MEEMAW. Hello.
TAMMY. It's me.
MEEMAW. And who is "me" exactly? I know a "Virginia" but
I never gave birth to any "Tammy".
TAMMY. Did you hear my records? Three of them went to #1.
MEEMAW. I don't have much time for the radio. Some of us
work all day. And then we sit sipping our lemonade on the Porch
all by our lonesome.
TAMMY. Well, MeeMaw, I'm working, too, to pay off Tina's
doctor bills. I'm on the road now with The George Jones Show, but
all this traveling's not good for the girls. *(Swallows her pride.)*
MeeMaw, they miss you. So I was wondering if they can stay with
you a little while, just 'till I get back. And MeeMaw, there's a man
I met who's a singer, too. His name's Don Chapel, and, well, I married him.

MEEMAW. Did you say George Jones?
DON. *(Entering)* Honey.
TAMMY. Don's here right now. I'm gonna put him on the phone.
DON. Hold on; we've got a problem. David Houston's manager wants to cut your set.
MEEMAW. *(Into phone.)* You mean "The" George Jones?
DON. He wants you to come out right now and sing the duet.
TAMMY. But that's not fair!

(MEE MAW shouts into phone as TAMMY hangs up.)

MEEMAW. George "The Possum" Jones?
TAMMY. Mee Maw; I've got to go. *(Hangs up.)*
MEEMAW. *(Looks at her glass.)* Oh Lord, I think my ice cubes melted.

(DAVID HUSTON'S MANAGER enters.)

HUSTON'S MANAGER. Make up your mind, girl. David Houston made you what you are, so if you don't sing when I tell you to, you don't use his band, either.
TAMMY. David Houston did not "make me". Billy Sherrill did.
HUSTON'S MANAGER. Well, everybody knows how Girl Singers 'make it' in this business anyhow.

(He laughs and TAMMY is furious. One of GEORGE JONES' "Jones Boys" Band, enters.)

JONES BOY. You want to keep it down out here? Me and George are trying to drink.

(TAMMY ignores him.)

TAMMY. *(To Huston's Manager.)* Mister, If you think I'm here because I slept with anybody, you are badly mistaken. And, if any "Girl Singer" had to sleep with you to sing with David, he'd be singing solo the rest of his life! *(She exits.)*

JONES BOY. She's got that right.

HUSTON'S MANAGER. Lady, you're not going on at all, cause you ain't got a band!

Winnipeg Concert

ANNOUNCER. *(Taped)* Ladies and Gentlemen, give a big, warm Winnipeg welcome to Mister George Jones.

(Music begins, lights up; Enormous applause. GEORGE JONES does not enter at first; Band members begin to look nervously off-stage as if he might be a "no-show". Finally, he enters.)

GEORGE. Hey, how are ya'll tonight? Sorry we're a little late, but I'll tell you what…I feel like singin' all night! If that's all right with all of you? *(Waits for audience response.)* Let's here it for the Jones Boys!

Song: *Love Bug*

GEORGE.
WELL I WAS RULING THE ROOST
AND I HAD ALL THE CHICKS TO MYSELF
AND THEN SUDDENLY IT HAPPENED
A FUNNY LITTLE FEELING I FELT
YEAH I TRIED TO OUTRUN IT
BUT IT FINALLY CAUGHT UP WITH ME
BUT HOW COULD I RUN FROM SOMETHING THAT I CAN'T
SEE?

OH - THAT - LITTLE BITTY TEENY WEENY THING
THEY CALL THE LOVE BUG
NOBODY'S EVER SEEN IT
BUT ITS GOT THE WHOLE WORLD SHOOK UP
IT ALL STARTED WITH A LITTLE BITTY KISS AND HUG
IT'S THE LITTLE BITTY TEENY WEENY THING
THEY CALL THE LOVE BUG

WELL I ALWAYS THOUGHT

I HAD ME A PRETTY GOOD STYLE
BUT I LOST THAT RACE
BY A GOOD OL' COUNTRY MILE
YEAH I WAS WALKING AROUND
WITH MY HEAD HELD WAY UP HIGH
AND THEN IT FOOLED ME, HIT ME
REALLY TOOK ME BY SURPRISE

OH - THAT - LITTLE BITTY TEENY WEENY THING
THEY CALL THE LOVE BUG
NOBODY'S EVER SEEN IT
BUT ITS GOT THE WHOLE WORLD SHOOK UP
IT ALL STARTED WITH A LITTLE BITTY KISS AND HUG
IT'S THE LITTLE BITTY TEENY WEENY THING
THEY CALL THE LOVE BUG
IT'S THE LITTLE BITTY TEENY WEENY THING
THEY CALL THE LOVE BUG.

GEORGE JONES. Thank you. You know I've recorded duets with a lot of ladies, Melba Montgomery, Margie Singleton; but there's a girl here tonight I'd rather sing with than anybody else in the world. She's got a big hit duet out right now with David Houston, but tonight I'd like to sing it with her. Let's see if we can get her out here…Ladies and Gentlemen, Miss Tammy Wynette.

(Applause. Beat. TAMMY comes from offstage. She stands facing her Idol, terrified, hands stiff at her side.)

GEORGE JONES. You might want to get a little closer to the microphone. *(Band begins to play. TAMMY walks stiffly to Jones' side. Low.)* Just have fun now. Relax.
TAMMY. *(Trying)* Okay.
GEORGE JONES. I don't know all the words.

(TAMMY freezes again.)

Song: *My Elusive Dreams*

TAMMY.
I FOLLOWED YOU TO TEXAS

I FOLLOWED YOU TO UTAH

GEORGE.
WE DIDN'T FIND IT THERE *(Pause)*

TAMMY. *(Prompting him.)*
"So we moved on"

GEORGE.
SO WE MOVED ON

TAMMY.
I FOLLOWED YOU TO ALABAM
THINGS LOOKED GOOD IN BIRMINGHAM

GEORGE.
WE DIDN'T FIND IT THERE

BOTH.
SO WE MOVED ON
I KNOW YOU'RE TIRED OF FOLLOWING
MY ELUSIVE DREAMS AND SCHEMES
FOR THEY'RE ONLY FLEETING THINGS
MY ELUSIVE DREAMS

TAMMY.
I HAD YOUR CHILD IN MEMPHIS

GEORGE.
You did?

TAMMY.
YOU HEARD OF WORK IN NASHVILLE

BOTH.
WE DIDN'T FIND IT THERE
SO WE MOVED ON

TAMMY.
I KNOW YOU'RE TIRED OF FOLLOWING
MY ELUSIVE DREAMS AND SCHEMES
FOR THEY'RE ONLY FLEETING THINGS
MY ELUSIVE DREAMS

TAMMY & GEORGE.
FOR THEY'RE ONLY FLEETING THINGS
MY ELUSIVE DREAMS

GEORGE.
Miss Tammy Wynette!

*(Applause; Lights change. The concert is over and EUPLE comes
to the edge of the stage, as TAMMY is getting ready to exit.)*

EUPLE. Wynette?! *(Tentatively)*
TAMMY. Euple. *(Surprised)* What are you doing here?
EUPLE. Heard you on the radio. And I said, "Hey". That's
you!
TAMMY. That's me.
EUPLE. *(Holds up a picture.)* They put this picture of you in
the Sunday paper. Some of the boys at work put it up on the wall. I
thought maybe you could sign it?
TAMMY. All right.
EUPLE. Kids are good?
TAMMY. *(With distance.)* The kids are fine. *(Signs it for him,
beat.)* You take care.
EUPLE. You, too. *(TAMMY exits. He reads the inscription out
loud.)* "Dream on, Baby. Dream on."

*(Lights down on EUPLE he exits, up on TAMMY catching up to
GEORGE JONES.)*

<u>Winnipeg – Backstage</u>

TAMMY. Oh, Mr. Jones. I can't tell you all how much I appre-
ciate what you did for me back there.
GEORGE. Look; I heard what happened. Nobody's going to
put you down on this tour if I can help it. I'll sing with you anytime.
TAMMY. Same here. I know the words to every song you ever
sung.
GEORGE. Oh do you?

GEORGE.
I TOOK A LITTLE SIP AND RIGHT AWAY I KNEW

TAMMY. *(Jumps in.)*
AS MY EYES BUGGED OUT AND MY FACE TURNED BLUE,

TAMMY AND GEORGE.
MIGHTY, MIGHTY PLEASIN' PAPPY'S CORN SQUEEZIN'

TAMMY.
SHHOOOH…WHITE LIGHTING.

GEORGE. That was an easy one…okay; try this…

GEORGE.
JUST BECAUSE I HAUNT THE SAME OLD PLACES
WHERE HER MEMORY LINGERS SO-

TAMMY. *(Interrupts)* That's wrong.
GEORGE. Wrong? Hell, it's my tune!

TAMMY.
WHERE THE MEM'RY OF HER LINGERS EV'RYWHERE

TAMMY/GEORGE.
JUST BECAUSE I'M NOT THE HAPPY GUY I USED TO BE

(DON CHAPEL enters, joins in the singing.)

TAMMY/GEORGE/DON.
SHE THINKS I…

*(Both TAMMY and GEORGE stop singing, GEORGE turns around
and give DON a look like, "who are you?)*

DON CHAPEL.
… STILL CARE.

DON CHAPEL. Great song. I'm a songwriter, too.
TAMMY. Mr. Jones…
GEORGE. George.
TAMMY. This is my husband, Don Chapel.

(They shake hands.)

DON CHAPEL. I've got some tunes in the car if you'd care to hear.

GEORGE. Sure I would. You folks are traveling by car?

TAMMY. We're saving up for a bus.

GEORGE. Well, I'm getting a new one, maybe you want to buy my old one. It needs a heater for the winter and it fries you in the summer, but it runs.

DON CHAPEL. How much are you asking?

TAMMY. *(As much to DON as GEORGE.)* We just put a down payment on a house. We can't really-

GEORGE. *(To TAMMY.)* For you, it's two thousand.

TAMMY. *(Stunned)* Only two? Are you sure?

DON. We'll take it.

GEORGE. You do that. See you later.

(GEORGE exits.)

DON CHAPEL. We've got a bus! I can't believe it!

TAMMY. *(Looking after GEORGE.)* I can't either.

DON CHAPEL. First thing tomorrow, I'm going to get our names painted on the side ten feet high from front to back. We are going to travel in style. I can see it now: *(He puts his arm around her.)* "The Don Chapel and Tammy Wynette Show".

(TAMMY looks to DON; not happy. Music begins, TAMMY begins singing "D-I-V-O-R-C-E" TAMMY crosses down center stage DON exits.)

Song: *D-I-V-O-R-C-E*

TAMMY.
OUR D-I-V-O-R-C-E BECOMES FINAL TODAY
ME AND LITTLE J-O-E WILL BE GOIN' AWAY
I LOVE YOU BOTH AND IT WILL BE PURE
    H-E-DOUBLE L FOR ME
OH, I WISH THAT WE COULD STOP THIS D-I-V-O-R-C-E

(A stranger walks up to the edge of the stage, holding out a photograph, TAMMY takes it, looks, and is flustered. Lights down from concert mode to TAMMY and DON'S home.)

<u>Kitchen Of Tammy And Don's Home</u>

(Music continues through the radio. TAMMY enters, overwhelmed. she holds the photo in a rage.)

TAMMY. Do you see this picture?

DON. You; doing exercises in the bedroom.

TAMMY. Doing exercises stark naked!

DON. You laughed when I took it.

TAMMY. I didn't laugh when some Man in the Audience gave it to me! How could he have gotten it? Did somebody break into our house?

DON. Tammy; don't get all worked up. You know photography's a hobby of mine. Sometimes I get names out of magazines and we swap pictures, that's all. Your name's not on it. Nobody can tell it's you.

TAMMY. That man could! Do you know how I felt? I felt like somebody hit me in the stomach; I wanted to die of shame. What kind of man would show somebody pictures of his own wife?

(Sound of Door Bell. TAMMY partially exits to answer the door and immediately returns to scene.)

TAMMY. Don; its George.

(GEORGE enters, he sings along with the music on the radio, he has had a few drinks.)

GEORGE.
MY D-I-V-O-R-C-E BECAME FINAL TODAY
(To TAMMY.) Did you hear that?

TAMMY. You sound great, George.

GEORGE. "MY D-I-V-O-R-C-E!"

TAMMY. George! You?

GEORGE. Me. And "It became final today"! Don, what have

you got to drink? We've got to make a toast.

(DON takes a bottle and two glasses out of the cabinet. GEORGE sits at the kitchen counter.)

DON. I'm happy to drink to divorce anytime.
TAMMY. Well, you can get some practice tonight because you're not sleeping with me.
DON. Don't you tell me what I'm doing.
TAMMY. I think what you did was inexcusable-
DON. I don't care what you think. Who'd want to sleep with a bitch like you anyway.

(GEORGE explodes, flipping over a chair. DON is terrified.)

GEORGE. You don't talk to her like that!
DON. What's it to you? She's my wife!
GEORGE. That may be so, but I'm in love with her. *(TAMMY is stunned. GEORGE walks over to her.)* And you love me, too, don't you?

(TAMMY looks at him, still in shock. Behind her in the distance, MEEMAW can be seen.)

MEEMAW. Wynette! Answer him!
TAMMY. Yes. Yes I do.
GEORGE. Okay, then. Let's gather up the children and go.

(GEORGE and TAMMY exit; DON stares after them, in astonishment.)

MEEMAW. *(To DON.)* Snap that, Shutterbug.

(Lights down on kitchen, up on hotel room.)

Nashville Hotel Suite

GEORGE. Girls all right?
TAMMY. I told them they could order anything from Room Service. They're in hog heaven.

GEORGE. That's good.
TAMMY. It is.

(Pause. Neither knows what to say.)

GEORGE. *(Pause)* You don't drink?
TAMMY. No.
GEORGE. Want to start? *(Tammy laughs.)* Tammy, you know; I fell in love with you the first time I heard you sing "Apartment #9".

TAMMY. I used to sing along with you all the time on the Radio. I can't believe-

(She turns away, overwhelmed.)

GEORGE. What's wrong?
TAMMY. How can George Jones, my idol, be in love with Virginia Wynette Pugh? I want to make you the happiest man alive. But I'm a pretty simple person.
GEORGE. That's a shame. Because I'm pretty sophisticated, myself.

(Music begins for "The Jet Set".)

TAMMY. You are?
GEORGE. Oh yeah. I'm part of the "In Crowd".
TAMMY. The "In Crowd"?
GEORGE. In-tense, In-destructible and In-toxicated.

Song: *(We're Not) The Jet Set*

GEORGE.
BY A FOUNTAIN BACK IN ROME
I FELL IN LOVE WITH YOU
IN A SMALL CAFÉ IN ATHENS
YOU SAID YOU LOVED ME TOO
AND IT WAS APRIL IN PARIS WHEN
I FIRST HELD YOU CLOSE TO ME
ROME, GEORGIA

TAMMY.
ATHENS, TEXAS

TAMMY AND GEORGE.
AND PARIS, TENNESSEE
NO, WE'RE NOT THE JET SET
WE'RE THE OLD CHEVROLET SET
THERE'S NO RIVIERA
IN FESTUS MISSOURI
AND YOU WON'T FIND ONASSIS
IN MULLINVILLE, KANSAS

ALL.
NO WE'RE NOT THE JET SET
WE'RE THE OLD CHEVROLET SET
BUT AIN'T WE GOT LOVE
NO, WE'RE NOT THE JET SET
WE'RE THE OLD CHEVRO-LET SET

TAMMY & GEORGE.
OUR STEAK AND MARTINIS

ALL.
IS DRAFT BEER AND WEENIES

TAMMY & GEORGE.
OUR BACH AND TCHAIKOVSKY

ALL.
IS HAGGARD AND HUSKY
NO WE'RE NOT THE JET SET
WE'RE THE OLD CHEVROLET SET
BUT AIN'T WE GOT LOVE
NO, WE'RE NOT THE JET SET
WE'RE THE OLD CHEVRO-LET SET

TAMMY & GEORGE.
THE JONES AND WYNETTE SET

ALL.
AIN'T THE FLAMING SUZETTE SET
OUR BACH AND TCHAIKOVSKY
IS HAGGARD AND HUSKY
NO WE'RE NOT THE JET SET
WE'RE THE OLD CHEVROLET SET
BUT AIN'T WE GOT LOVE
NO WE'RE NOT THE JET SET
WE'RE THE OLD CHEVROLET SET
BUT AIN'T WE GOT LOVE

(GEORGE and TAMMY kiss and disappear behind the company.)

MEEMAW. *(Leaving the company and exiting.)* Third Time's a charm.

(Lights go down on hotel suite and come up in a hospital. TAMMY is seated at the edge of the bed with her new baby in her arms.)

Hospital 1970

GEORGE. Honey, you don't know how happy you made me. She's the prettiest little thing in the whole nursery.
TAMMY. Look at these brown eyes. This girl is a Jones.
GEORGE. You think so?
TAMMY. Sure I do. Her eyes, her hair, even her little fingers. She looks just like her daddy.

(MEEMAW enters.)

MEEMAW. Billy Sherrill's here. He brought the baby a recording contract.
GEORGE. I'll go get him.

(GEORGE exits.)

TAMMY. Did George tell you about the Opry?
MEEMAW. He did.
TAMMY. *(Thrilled)* I can't believe I'm going to sing on the

same stage Hank Williams and Patsy Cline did. And you know what? I don't even have to twirl a baton.

(Lights up on GEORGE on telephone.)

GEORGE. *(Thrilled)* Mama, Her name is Tamala Georgette. She's got my eyes, my hair, even my fingers. *(Pause)* Of course she's beautiful! She looks just like me.

(Lights down on GEORGE, up on.)

<u>Ryman Auditorium – Grand Ol' Opry – 1971</u>

ANNOUNCER. Welcome back to the Grand Ol' Opry. This portion of our show is brought to you by Maxwell House Coffee and Beechnut Chewing Tobacco. Coming up on the 'Opry next week will be Little Jimmie Dickens, Jack Green and the Jolly Green Giants, Porter Wagoner and the Wagonmasters, Billy Walker and Jeanie Seely, Roy Pillow and Charlie Walker. And appearing on this stage for the first time, The Can't Hardly Playboys. And folks, while you're here be sure to pick up your Grand Ol' Opry Autograph Picture Books and a seat cushion. Remember: Be kind to your behind. But right now I'd like to tip my hat to the sponsors making it possible for us to be with you tonight: Liberty Mutual Insurance and our good friend Martha White.

COUNTRY TRIO.
WELL YOU BAKE RIGHT
WITH MARTHA WHITE (YES MA'AM!)
GOODNESS GRACIOUS GOOD AND LIGHT
MISS MARTHA WHITE
YOU BAKE BETTER BISCUITS CAKES AND PIES
WITH MARTHA WHITE'S SELF-RISING FLOUR,
THAT ONE ALL-PURPOSE FLOUR,
MARTHA WHITE'S SELF-RISING FLOUR'S
GOT "HOT RISE"

ANNOUNCER. Since 1899, when Richard Lindsey first named his flour after his little daughter, Martha, the best cooks you know rely on Martha White for easy baked foods with down home Southern flavor.

COUNTRY TRIO.
WITH MARTHA WHITE'S SELF-RISING FLOUR,
THAT ONE ALL-PURPOSE FLOUR,
MARTHA WHITE'S SELF-RISING FLOUR'S
GOT "HOT RISE"

ONE OF COUNTRY TRIO.
Goodness gracious, it's good!

(Applause)

ANNOUNCER. *(Taped)* WSM is proud to introduce our two newest members of the Grand Ol' Opry: Mister George Jones and Miss Tammy Wynettte.

(Crowd applause; Lights up, TAMMY and GEORGE enter for up center and cross down stage to center.)

Song: *Near You*

GEORGE.
THERE'S JUST ONE PLACE FOR ME,

TAMMY AND GEORGE.
NEAR YOU

TAMMY.
IT'S LIKE HEAVEN TO BE

TAMMY AND GEORGE.
NEAR YOU

GEORGE.
TIMES WHEN WE'RE APART
I CAN'T FACE MY HEART

> **TAMMY.**
> SAY YOU'LL NEVER STRAY
>
> **TAMMY.**
> MORE THAN TWO LIPS AWAY
>
> **GEORGE.**
> IF MY HOURS COULD BE SPENT,
>
> **TAMMY AND GEORGE.**
> NEAR YOU
>
> **TAMMY.**
> I'D BE MORE THAN CONTENT,
>
> **TAMMY AND GEORGE.**
> NEAR YOU
>
> **TAMMY.**
> MAKE MY LIFE WORTH WHILE
> BY TELLING ME THAT I'LL
>
> **TAMMY & GEORGE.**
> SPEND THE REST OF MY DAYS, NEAR YOU,
> SPEND THE REST OF MY DAYS, NEAR YOU

(Applause from audience.)

TAMMY. Thank you. You know, George and I have been blessed with so many wonderful changes in our lives. Marriage, our new baby.

GEORGE. That's right. Thanks to Tammy, George Jones has turned in to a regular homebody.

TAMMY. And on the nights George finds his way home, we couldn't be happier.

Song: *We're Gonna Hold On*

> **GEORGE.**
> WE'RE GONNA HOLD ON

TAMMY AND GEORGE.
WE'RE GONNA HOLD ON
WE'RE GONNA HOLD ON AND ON
TO EACH OTHER

LIFE CAN BE ROUGH
SOMETIMES IT'S KIND
A REAL GOOD LIFE
IS HARD TO FIND

BUT THE BEST LOVE
IS THE LOVE WE'VE KNOWN
AND THE FAITH WE HAVE BETWEEN US
MAKES IT GROW

(Lights down.)

Landmark Hotel – Las Vegas

ANNOUNCER. Tonight, the Landmark Hotel in Las Vegas presents Mr. and Mrs. Country Music.

(Lights up backstage, TAMMY huddles with two JONES BOYS.)

JONES BOY ONE. We can't find George. We had a couple of drinks on the plane, but he wasn't anywhere near drunk. When we got off to change planes that's the last we saw him.

JONES BOY TWO. He's scared to death to face a Vegas audience. He thinks they'll hate him because he's so country.

TAMMY. You've got to find him.

JONES BOY ONE. We will. But not tonight. You'll have to go on alone.

TAMMY. I can't do that!

JONES BOY TWO. You've got no choice. That's a sold out show out there.

JONES BOY. Tammy; don't worry. You'll do just fine. *(Kisses her cheek.)* And Happy Birthday.

(Lights up on a nervous TAMMY into concert mode.)

Song: *We're Gonna Hold On*

TAMMY.
SOME LOVE LIVES
AND SOME LOVE DON'T
      (TAMMY realizes what's she said.)
WE'VE GOT THE KIND OF LOVE WE WANT
IT BRINGS US HAPPINESS
ALL THROUGH THE DAY
      (Upset, fights to finish.)
AND NOTHING CAN EVER
MAKE IT -

(TAMMY can't finish; Quickly walks off stage.)

*(Lights go down on concert, TAMMY exits. GEORGE enters
      singing.)*

<u>Tammy and George's Home In Nashville - 1975</u>

GEORGE.
WE'RE GONNA HOLD ON
WE'RE GONNA HOLD ON
THERE GONNA HOLD ON
TO EACH OTHER

*(Lights up on GEORGE & TAMMY'S kitchen; months later the
      table's piled with dirty dishes. GEORGE enters with flowers.
      He has been "out". He tries to give them to TAMMY, who will
      not take them.)*

GEORGE. Honey-
TAMMY. Don't say it, George. "Sorry" doesn't mean a thing
anymore. "I promise" is a joke.
GEORGE. It won't happen again.
TAMMY. You said that after Vegas. And the Hospital. Look at
this house!
GEORGE. We had a little party-
TAMMY. You and what army? You can't walk without trip-

ping over whiskey bottles. Garbage, cigarette butts and that sink's got a mountain of dirty dishes.

GEORGE. I'll clean it all up. I promise. But I can't now. I'm so sick I've got to have something to settle my stomach.

TAMMY. All right, I'll fix you something.

GEORGE. Thank you. Thank you, Tammy.

(GEORGE sits down, exhausted. TAMMY puts a plate before him.)

TAMMY. Here's some moldy beans and rotten meat and stale cornbread that's been out for days.

GEORGE. Don't do this to me-

TAMMY. Don't do this to me and your family! George, it's either us or the liquor. If you can't give it up, I'm giving up on you.

Song: *Hold On (Reprise)*

GEORGE.
TIME WILL TELL *(Spoken)*
IF YOU'RE RIGHT OR WRONG

GEORGE AND TAMMY.
WE KNOW WE'RE RIGHT BY HOLDING ON
AND THE FUTURE IS SET FOR YOU AND ME
FILLED WITH LOVE THE WAY WE WANT IT TO BE
WE'RE GONNA HOLD ON

MEEMAW. That's how you remember it?

TAMMY. It's the truth.

MEEMAW. Part of it. But how about you? When were you going to give up your Valium and your Demerol?

TAMMY. When the pain stopped. You know I had an appendectomy. And operations for the scar tissue; it never healed right-

MEEMAW. Nothing can heal if you don't take time to rest.

TAMMY. When could I have done that? I was always making up for the concerts George missed!

MEEMAW. That was your choice.

TAMMY. Why are you doing this to me?

MEEMAW. I'm trying to help you see the truth-

TAMMY. The truth is, you never said a word to me back then. Now, all of a sudden you know everything?

MEEMAW. That's right. I'm a genius looking backwards.

(Beds slide out. Music. We hear a spare, sad arrangement of "Stand By Your Man" underscoring the scene. GEORGE takes out a bottle and glass and sits on the of one bed, puts the bottle on the floor. TAMMY takes out a bottle of pills and sits on the other bed. He and TAMMY talk; two people not able to really hear what the other is saying.)

TAMMY. I don't know what's funnier; the fact that it took fifteen minutes for Billy and I to write my biggest hit or that it's called "Stand By Your Man".

GEORGE. Tammy, are you going to love me when I'm old?

TAMMY. I'm a failure. As a wife. As A lover. Maybe if I could keep you happier at home. Maybe if I was smarter or prettier or sexier you'd stop drinking. I don't know who you are trying to escape, me or you.

GEORGE. When Georgette was born I was sober over a year. You remember that? It was hard, but I did it. A whole year without a drop. That's like a three-legged horse winning the Kentucky Derby.

TAMMY. I don't know how to help you. You nip, I nag.

GEORGE. I hated my Daddy for his drinking. I hated him for the miserable life he gave my Momma. But here I am doing the same thing. It just doesn't make any sense.

(GEORGE takes a drink.)

TAMMY. The King and Queen of Country Music. People love that. They want that. So do I.

(TAMMY takes a pill.)

GEORGE. Sometimes I wonder, what if I did stop? You see what people throw onstage; beer and booze and every kind of drug. I pick them up and the crowd cheers. They even cheer when I don't show up; then they buy their "I've Seen No Show Jones" shirts.

That's the George Jones they're paying to see – or not see. The drinking Jones, the fighting Jones. *(TAMMY lies down on the bed, GEORGE doesn't notice.)* I wouldn't be George Jones without it. And who'd pay to see me then? (Music stops.) Tammy; I Love you. Tammy?

(But TAMMY is now asleep on the bed. GEORGE rises, crosses over to her, takes the bottle of pills puts it on the night stand; covers her with a blanket and kisses her gently. He exits. Lights up the next morning. MEEMAW enters.)

MEEMAW. Tammy, Tammy. His car's gone. What do you want me to do?

TAMMY. Start packing. We promised the girls a Christmas vacation and I'm not going to disappoint them.

MEEMAW. We should wait to hear. Maybe he'll meet us-

TAMMY. I'm leaving George.

MEEMAW. *(Pause)* You can't do that.

TAMMY. I have to.

MEEMAW. Have to what? Run away like you always do?

TAMMY. I tried, MeeMaw, you know I did. Over and over-

MEEMAW. You think your Daddy and me didn't have our problems? Sometimes you just have to live with them.

TAMMY. The girls don't. I can't let them grow up like this.

MEEMAW. Maybe you're the one who should grow up!

TAMMY. Why me, MeeMaw? Why me and not him?

MEEMAW. Because he's George Jones!

TAMMY. And who am I? Just once I'd like you to say, "She's Tammy Wynette. She's my daughter." Cause you know what, MeeMaw? I sing, too. I know that doesn't mean much to you, but it does to me.

MEEMAW. I know what it means to you. More than anything. Or anybody.

GEORGETTE. *(Offstage)* Mommy!

MEEMAW. Don't worry. I'll take care of her.

(Music starts as MEEMAW exits.)

Song: *I Still Believe In Fairy Tales*

TAMMY.
I BELIEVE IN FAIRY TALES
WHERE KNIGHTS IN SHINING ARMOR COME ALONG
YOU WERE MY KNIGHT IN SHINING ARMOR
AND YOU STOLE MY HEART WITH A SONG

YOU GAVE ME A CASTLE AND A PRINCESS
AND I WAS THE WORLD'S PROUDEST QUEEN
AND THEN CAME THAT DRAGON IN THE BOTTLE
AND I WATCHED AS IT SLOWLY SLAYED THE KING

(Lights up on GEORGE holding a phone.)

GEORGE. I'm not going to lie to you. I've been drinking. But I got a room in Franklin and slept it off. I'll be coming home soon.
TAMMY. No, George. You're not coming home. Never again.

(TAMMY hangs up. Lights fade on GEORGE. She takes center stage, summoning up all her courage, determined to go on. She is now performing in concert.)

Song: *I Still Believe In Fairy Tales*

TAMMY.
AND WE ALL LIVED HAPPY NEVER AFTER
FOR WE JUST PUT THE CASTLE UP FOR SALE
BUT I GUESS THAT I WILL ALWAYS BE A DREAMER
FOR I STILL BELIEVE IN FAIRY TALES

I STILL BELIEVE IN FAIRY TALES

(TAMMY exits.)

END OF ACT ONE

ACT II

<u>Alabama Concert</u>

ANNOUNCER. Ladies and Gentleman, the First Lady of Country Music: Tammy Wynette.

(Lights up; a nervous TAMMY comes on stage for her first "solo" show without GEORGE.)

TAMMY. *(Apprehensive)* Thank you. I am happy to be back in Alabama-
VOICE FROM CROWD. *(Prerecorded, shouts.)* Where's George?
TAMMY. *(Trying to ignore it.)* This is a song I love. I hope you do, too.
SECOND VOICE. Where's George Jones?

(TAMMY is frozen. The JONES BOYS stop playing. A JONES BOY calls to the AUDIENCE.)

JONES BOY. She doesn't know where George is! Even George doesn't know where George is.

Song: *Another Chance*

TAMMY.
WHEN   YOU LEFT SAID YOU WAS DOIN' ME A FAVOR
I CRIED AND I BEGGED YOU NOT TO GO

NOW IT'S BEEN TWO SHORT WEEKS
AND YOU'RE WANTIN' TO COME BACK
WELL I THINK THERE'S SOMETHING
THAT YOU OUGHT TO KNOW

WELL I'VE REARRANGED THE LIVING ROOM TO SUIT ME
I GAVE YOUR FAVORITE CHAIR TO CHARITY
THAT CLOSET YOU INSISTED ON, IT'S MINE NOW
SO DON'T BRING YOUR OL' HANGUPS BACK TO ME

CAUSE I'M WEARING MY JEANS A LITTLE BIT TIGHTER
CHANGED MY HAIRSTYLE AND I'M LEARNING HOW TO
DANCE
SO BABY YOU BEST WAIT A LITTLE BIT LONGER
'FORE YOU COME BACK AND GIVE ME ANOTHER
CHANCE

    TAMMY. Ladies and Gentlemen, let me introduce the best band in the world: Formerly the Jones Boys, now the Country Gentlemen. They're my half of the property settlement. *(Laughter)* The truth is that even though George and I couldn't live with each other, I still think he's the Greatest Singer in Country Music.

    TAMMY.
I THANK YOU FOR YOUR CALL
BUT SOMEONE'S KNOCKING AT MY DOOR
AND HE'S DRIVING A BIG OL' CADILLAC
I PROB'LY WON'T BE HOME
WHEN YOU COME TO GET YOUR CLOTHES
THEY'RE ON THE FRONT PORCH IN A PAPER SACK

YEAH I'M WEARING MY JEANS A LITTLE BIT TIGHTER
CHANGED MY HAIRSTYLE AND I'M LEARNING HOW TO
DANCE
SO BABY YOU BEST WAIT A LITTLE BIT LONGER
'FORE YOU COME BACK AND GIVE ME ANOTHER
CHANCE

THANKS ANYWAY, DON'T NEED ANOTHER CHANCE

THINK I'LL PASS

TAMMY. Thank you so much! You don't know how much it means to me. *(Intro music to "Till I Can Make It On My Own")* I'd like to sing you a song I just finished; you'll be the first beside my girls to hear it.

Song: *Till I Can Make It On My Own*

TAMMY.
I'LL NEED TIME TO GET YOU OFF MY MIND
AND I MAY SOMETIMES BOTHER YOU
TRY TO BE IN TOUCH WITH YOU
EVEN ASK TOO MUCH OF YOU FROM TIME TO TIME

NOW AND THEN
LORD YOU KNOW I'LL NEED A FRIEND
TILL I GET USED TO LOSING YOU
LET ME KEEP ON USING YOU
ILL I CAN MAKE IT ON MY OWN

I'LL GET BY
BUT NO MATTER HOW I TRY
THERE'LL BE TIMES YOU KNOW I'LL CALL
CHANCES ARE MY TEARS WILL FALL
AND I'LL HAVE NO PRIDE AT ALL
FROM TIME TO TIME

(Lights up on GEORGE JONES working on his own new song.)

GEORGE JONES.
JUST BECAUSE I HAUNT THE SAME OLD PLACES
WHERE THE MEMORY OF HER LINGERS EVERYWHERE

TAMMY.
SURELY SOMEDAY I'LL LOOK UP AND SEE THE MORNING
SUN
WITHOUT ANOTHER LONELY NIGHT BEHIND ME
THEN I'LL KNOW I'M OVER YOU AND ALL MY CRYIN'S

DONE
NO MORE HURTIN' MEMORIES CAN FIND ME
BUT TILL THEN
LORD YOU KNOW I'M GONNA NEED A FRIEND
TILL I GET USED TO LOSING YOU
LET ME KEEP ON USING YOU
TILL I CAN MAKE IT ON MY OWN

    GEORGE.
JUST BECAUSE I"M NOT THE HAPPY GUY I USED TO BE

    TAMMY.
TILL I CAN MAKE IT ON MY OWN

    GEORGE.
SHE THINKS I STILL CARE.

    TAMMY.
ON MY OWN

(Song concludes. TAMMY turns to MEEMAW; They are now in the present.)

<u>Limbo</u>

    TAMMY. I was so afraid of being out there all alone like that.
    MEEMAW. You were no different off stage. You never once finished the sentence "I'm single again" before the boys were knocking on your door like woodpeckers. And that's the way you liked it.
    TAMMY. Did I?
    MEE MAW. You couldn't stand being by yourself. Never could; you know I'm right. Tell me this, Virginia Pugh, what was so petrifying about being alone?
    TAMMY. The thought you'd come over.

(Sound of knock on door.)

    MEE MAW. Next!

(Light's up on TAMMY'S nashville home. BURT REYNOLDS enters.)

<u>Tammy's Nashville Home</u>

BURT. Well, I knew you were gonna look good, but I didn't know you'd look this damn good.

TAMMY. Thank you. *(Nervous laughter.)*

BURT. We're going to meet Jerry Reed and Priscilla at Mario's if that's all right.

TAMMY. Sure it is, but why don't you come in and meet my family, first.

(TAMMY'S daughter enters in robe with towel over head.)

TAMMY. This is my daughter Tina. Tina, come over and meet Burt Reynolds.

(TINA, stunned, realizing who it is screams and runs off.)

BURT. Nice to meet you, Tina.

TAMMY. MeeMaw-

MEEMAW. *(Looks up, loses her breath.)* Bless my heart it's the Bandit! (Pump – hand shakes him vigorously.)

BURT. MeeMaw, nice to meet you. That's quite a handshake you've got there. Don't tell me you read that trashy magazine, too. My mother does the same thing. I caught her reading a story about me last week and I said, 'Mama, you know those stories aren't true.' And she said, 'Yes, but it's a good picture, Son."

(MEEMAW and TAMMY laugh.)

MEEMAW. Burt, are you married?

TAMMY. We've got to go.

BURT. *(To MEEMAW.)* Good night-

(TAMMY pulls him out.)

MEEMAW. Thank you, Jesus!

BURT. Take my car?

<u>Burt's Car</u>

TAMMY. All right.
BURT. Radio?

(Music: Introduction to "Did You Ever".)

BURT. This is your song, isn't it?
TAMMY. George and I sang it.
BURT. If you sing along, we'll have stereo.
TAMMY. Only if you sing, too.
BURT. I can't sing!
TAMMY. Prove it.
BURT. I did. In "Best Little Whorehouse".
TAMMY. Come on, now; jump in.

Song: *Did You Ever*

BURT.
TAMMY DID YOU EVER

TAMMY.
NOT SO MUCH THAT YOU COULD NOTICE

BURT.
WELL COULD YOU ESTIMATE HOW MANY

TAMMY.
EIGHT OR NINE

BURT.
WELL, WILL YOU DO IT ANYMORE

TAMMY.
AS SOON AS YOU WALK OUT THE DOOR

BURT.
YEAH, I JUST WONDERED DID YOU EVER

TAMMY.
ALL THE TIME
COULD I FIX YOU ONE SMALL

BURT.
NO THANKS I JUST HAD ONE

TAMMY.
THEN HOW ABOUT A NICE BIG
BURT.
WELL, THAT WOULD BE JUST FINE

TAMMY.
IS THERE ANY SPECIAL WAY

BURT.
OH NO WHATEVER YOU SAY

TAMMY.
I JUST WONDERED HAVE YOU EVER

BURT.
ALL THE TIME

(SOUND of police siren. TAMMY looks into the rear mirror.)

TAMMY. That's a police car.
BURT. I'm pulling over.

(OFFICER comes forward holding a ticket book.)

BURT. Evening, Officer.
OFFICER. Boy, do you have any idea... Hey aren't you Burt Reynolds?
BURT. Yes, Sir.
OFFICER. Could I get an autograph?
BURT. You bet.
OFFICER. I've seen every one of your movies. Except that one, "Deliverance". *(Shudders)* Had to walk out. Every time since I hear a pig squeal I reach for my gun. Drive safe now, you hear.

(Takes autograph, tips his hat, starts to exit, song resumes.)

TAMMY. Weeeeeeeeee!!!! *(Squeals like a pig at the police officer as a joke. The officer jumps.)*

BURT.
DOES HE LOOK LIKE

TAMMY.
NO HE'S TALLER AND MORE HANDSOME

BURT.
WELL IS HE AS OLD

TAMMY.
OH NO HE'S YOUNG AND IN HIS PRIME

BURT.
DOES YOUR MOTHER KNOW I'LL BET

TAMMY.
OH NO I HAVEN'T TOLD YOU YET

BURT.
WELL I JUST WONDERED DO YOU EVER

TAMMY.
ALL THE TIME

BOTH.
I JUST WONDERED DID YOU EVER
ALL THE TIME

(Song ends, they kiss. Light's down on TAMMY & BURT, MEEMAW enters light, TAMMY crosses into light.)

<u>Limbo</u>

MEEMAW. And as the Painted Horse said to the Merry Go Round, "Here we go again."

TAMMY. I like to be in a relationship. Since when is falling in love a bad thing?

MEEMAW. Falling in love is easy. Staying in love is the tricky part.

TAMMY. I never married Burt.

MEEMAW. Did he ask you?

TAMMY. That's not fair.

MEEMAW. So he didn't. Well, that other one you were seeing made up for it. That rich, good looking, Mercedes driving fella.

TAMMY. Michael Tomlin.

MEEMAW. He was bad as you. "So Tammy would you like to go to a movie, to dinner, or get married? All three? Well, heck, why not"

(Light change.)

ALL.
Tammy! Tammy! Tammy!

NATIONAL ENQUIRER REPORTER ONE. Tammy! National Enquirer! What's your relationship with Burt?

NATIONAL ENQUIRER REPORTER TWO. Why did you buy a house so close to Reynolds's ranch?

STAR REPORTER ONE. What does Jones think of this?

NATIONAL ENQUIRER REPORTER ONE. Are you and Burt engaged?

STAR REPORTER ONE. Do you ever think of Jones?

NATIONAL ENQUIRER REPORTER TWO. Are you and Burt getting married?

TAMMY. No!

NATIONAL ENQUIRER REPORTER ONE/TWO. Why not?

TAMMY. Because I'm marrying Michael Tomlin.

Limbo – Marriage To Michael Tomlin

(Lights up TAMMY double, walking onstage to marry MICHAEL TOMLIN. As GEORGE and TAMMY sing "Golden Ring".)

D.J. *(Prerecorded)* The number one record in Nashville, together again at least in song, Tammy Wynette and George Jones.

Song: *Golden Ring*

TAMMY.
IN A PAWN SHOP IN CHICAGO ON A SUNNY SUMMER DAY
A COUPLE GAZES AT THE WEDDING RINGS THERE ON
   DISPLAY

GEORGE.
SHE SMILES AND NODS HER HEAD AS HE SAYS,
HONEY THAT'S FOR YOU
IT'S NOT MUCH BUT IT'S THE BEST THAT I CAN DO

BOTH.
GOLDEN RING, WITH ONE TINY LITTLE STONE
WAITING THERE FOR SOMEONE TO TAKE IT HOME
BY ITSELF IT'S JUST A COLD METALLIC THING
ONLY LOVE CAN MAKE A GOLDEN WEDDING RING

TAMMY.
IN A LITTLE WEDDING CHAPEL LATER ON THAT AFTER
NOON
AN OLD UPRIGHT PIANO PLAYS THAT OLD FAMILIAR
TUNE

GEORGE.
TEARS ROLL DOWN HER CHEEKS AND HAPPY THOUGHTS
RUN
THROUGH HER HEAD
AS HE WHISPERS LOW WITH THIS RING I THEE WED

BOTH.
GOLDEN RING
WITH ONE TINY LITTLE STONE
SHINING RING – NOW AT LAST IT'S FOUND A HOME
BY ITSELF IT'S JUST A COLD METALLIC THING
ONLY LOVE CAN MAKE A GOLDEN WEDDING RING

REVEREND. If anyone among us objects to the union of Tammy and Michael, speak now or forever hold your peace.

(MEEMAW stands as to object to the wedding and TAMMY gives her a "stop" gesture.)

TAMMY.
IN A SMALL TWO ROOM APARTMENT AS THEY FIGHT THEIR
FINAL ROUND
HE SAYS YOU WON'T ADMIT IT BUT I KNOW YOU'RE LEAVING TOWN
GEORGE.
SHE SAYS ONE THING'S FOR CERTAIN, I DON'T LOVE YOU ANYMORE
AND THROWS DOWN THE RING AS SHE WALKS OUT THE DOOR

(As the ceremony is over, MICHAEL TOMLIN and TAMMY double, cross down stage and go into the audience to greet them as guests at their wedding. They exit up the center aisle of the the-atre.)

ALL.
GOLDEN RING
WITH ONE TINY LITTLE STONE
CAST ASIDE – LIKE THE LOVE THAT'S DEAD AND GONE
BY ITSELF IT'S JUST A COLD METALLIC THING
ONLY LOVE CAN MAKE A GOLDEN WEDDING RING

TAMMY & GEORGE.
IN A PAWN SHOP IN CHICAGO ON A SUNNY SUMMER DAY
A COUPLE GAZES AT THE WEDDING RINGS THERE ON DISPLAY

ALL.
GOLDEN RING

(During the following song TAMMY sings to GEORGE.)

Song: *You And Me*

TAMMY.
I CAN HEAR THE RAIN IT'S FALLING SOFTLY
AS I WATCH HIM LYING NEXT TO ME
I CAN FEEL HIS HEART IS BEATING SOFTLY
HE JUST LOVED ME SO TENDERLY
BUT IT SHOULD BE YOU AND ME

SO I'LL JUST CLOSE MY EYES AND DREAM ABOUT YOU
CAUSE VERY TIME I DREAM YOU'RE ALWAYS THERE
THEN YOU'LL LOCK THE DOOR BEHIND US
IN MY DREAMS THE WORLD CAN'T FIND US
IT WILL BE SO REAL TO ME
IT'S FINALLLY YOU AND ME

(Light's down on TAMMY.)

Song: *If Drinking Don't Kill Me (Her Memory Will)*

GEORGE.
THE BARS ARE ALL CLOSED
IT'S FOUR IN THE MORNING
MUST HAVE SHUT 'EM ALL DOWN
BY THE SHAPE THAT I'M IN
I LAY MY HEAD ON THE WHEEL
AND THE HORN BEGINS HONKING
THE WHOLE NEIGHBORHOOD KNOWS
THAT I'M HOME DRUNK AGAIN

AND IF DRINKING DON'T' KILL ME
HER MEMORY WILL
I CAN'T HOLD OUT MUCH LONGER
THE WAY THAT I FEEL
WITH THE BLOOD FROM MY BODY
I COULD START MY OWN STILL
AND IF DRINKING DON'T KILL ME
HER MEMORY WILL

AND IF DRINKING DON'T KILL ME,
THEN TAMMY'S MEMORY WILL.

Hospital Waiting Room

(Lights up on GEORGE; MEEMAW enters.)

GEORGE. Meemaw!

MEEMAW. *(Noticing him.)* George!

GEORGE. I went by the house; how is she?

MEEMAW. She's sleeping now. Just got out of surgery. Third surgery in just over a year. First her kidney, then her adhesions, now her gall bladder. That girl should up and marry a doctor.

GEORGE, I hear she and Michael Tomlin –

MEEMAW. You heard right. Forty-four days and she asked for an annulment. I've boiled eggs longer –

GEORGE. And I ate them.

MEEMAW. I swear that girl just drives me around the bend. She never said she was feeling so poorly. I ran all over the house calling for her, then I found her unconscious on the bathroom floor. I thought...I thought...

(MEE MAW turns away, overcome; GEORGE comforts her.)

GEORGE. She'll be just fine.

MEE MAW. I know that. It's just the vapors in this hospital.

GEORGE. Tell me, does Tammy still bite her nails?

MEEMAW. Big time. Why?

GEORGE. More or less than when we were married?

MEEMAW. More, I'd say. What does that mean?

GEORGE. Aw, probably nothing. Everybody's got their bad habits. Some folks bite their nails; some people drive their lawn mowers into town.

MEEMAW. George, it's good of you to come.

GEORGE. *(Waves it off.)* Ah...

MEEMAW. It is. I miss you. So do the girls.

GEORGE. Some days, I miss me, too.

(Lights fade in waiting room and come up in TAMMY'S hospital room. Sound of knock on her door. TAMMY wakes.)

Hospital Room

TAMMY. Come in. *(BURT REYNOLDS enters.)* Burt!

BURT. Don't get up. I couldn't decide whether to bring flowers or magazines, so I wrote a poem instead.

TAMMY. You wrote a poem?

BURT. I wrote a poem. It's in crayon, but it rhymes.

TAMMY. Read it to me.

BURT. All right then. Brace yourself.

"I once knew a lady named Tammy
Who had an old-fashioned daddy and mammy,
At one time she had to pick cotton,
For which she has long since forgotten,
Now she's grown up with kids of her own.
Got a big shining bus, two houses, twelve phones
She's pretty and smart, can even write charts
But what's best is this beauty's big heart
Sometimes she's sick and she stumbles
Sometimes she's mad and she grumbles
Nobody loves what's perfect
This don't rhyme, but who gives a shit."

(TAMMY laughs.) Why'd you do it, Tammy? Why'd you get married?

TAMMY. I don't know. It was like dating that got out of hand.

BURT. We can't have a real friendship if we're going to play games and not be honest with each other. I want to have the kind of relationship where you can tell me about any other man in your life, and if I've met somebody important to me, you'd be the first to know.

TAMMY. That's what I want, too.

BURT. All right, then. Happy Divorce.

(Music begins. BURT kisses her and leaves the room. Lights out on hospital room and come up in a recording studio.)

<u>Recording Studio</u>

Song: *Till I Get It Right*

TAMMY.
I'LL JUST KEEP ON FALLING IN LOVE
TILL I GET IT RIGHT
BUT NOW I'M LIKE A WOUNDED BIRD HUNGRY FOR THE
SKY
BUT IF I TRIED MY WINGS AND TRIED LONG ENOUGH
I'M BOUND TO LEARN TO FLY
SO I'LL JUST KEEP ON FALLING IN LOVE
'TILL I GET IT RIGHT

(TAMMY calls to offstage engineer.)

TAMMY. John, can I take a minute?
JOHN. *(Offstage)* Sure, Tammy. Guys, let's run it down from the top. 1,2,3…
RICHEY. Hey, Tammy.
TAMMY. Richey.

(Music, low, underscoring the scene.)

TAMMY. I'm so sorry to hear about you and Sheila.
RICHEY. Three years we were married.
TAMMY. Beats my record; I didn't last three months.
RICHEY. Probably all for the best.
TAMMY. I believe that. There's nothing wrong with being on your own.
RICHEY. That's true.
TAMMY. Especially when you've got good friends around you.
RICHEY. And Tammy, you know, anything you need-
TAMMY. The same here Richey. You know that. Anything.

(Awkward pause.)

RICHEY. Well, I'd better be getting. I'm down the hall. Studio B.

TAMMY. All right.

RICHEY. *(Starts to go; stops.)* Unless you wanted to go across the street; get something to eat or drink?

TAMMY. Richey; can you wait-

RICHEY. You're right! I'm sorry. It just came out. The last thing either of us should be doing is rushing into anything. Tammy, we're friends and I hope we always will be. Good, friendly friends.

(Almost going to kiss her on the cheek, but puts out his hand instead.)

TAMMY. What I meant was, can you wait until the sessions over?

RICHEY. Sure, I'll be waiting.

JOHN. *(O.S.)* Tammy, we're gonna take it from the bridge.

TAMMY. Sure thing.

(Band begins to play, TAMMY steps up to the microphone. RICHEY sits and watches end of session.)

TAMMY.
IF PRACTICE MAKES PERFECT
THEN I'M NEAR BOUT AS PERFECTAS I'LL BE IN MY LIFE
SO I'LL JUST KEEP ON FALLING IN LOVE
TILL I GET IT RIGHT

(Lights down for RICHEY to exit; up on MEEMAW and TAMMY.)

Limbo

MEEMAW. I never should have let you out of my sight without a chaperone and an ambulance.

TAMMY. Richey was different.

MEEMAW. Like the Number Five's different from the Number Four. Though I have to say he's the only man I ever saw wear a short sleeve tuxedo.

TAMMY. Richey is a brilliant musician, a great songwriter and he loves me. He took over all the business and managed my whole career.

MEEMAW. I know he did. But that wasn't the only thing that needed managing.

TAMMY. *(Frustrated)* Why are you doing this to me?

MEEMAW. I told you, honey. You've got to be able to look back and see yourself, true and clear. No matter what happened to you. Or no matter what didn't.

(Lights fade.)

ANCHORMAN. *(Recorded)* Tammy Wynette was kidnapped in broad daylight today from the parking lot of the Green Hills Mall-

ANCHORWOMAN. *(Recorded)* Held at gunpoint by a Masked Man in her back seat, Wynette drove her Yellow Cadillac for hours until they were joined by a reported Accomplice-

ANCHORMAN. Wynette was pushed out of her car after her Assailant wrapped a stocking around her neck and struck her in the face-

ANCHORWOMAN. Both Wynette and her sedan were abandoned-

ANCHORMAN. Mr. Bobby Young found the stumbling Wynette at the roadside near his driveway.

(Lights up on side stage.)

BOBBY YOUNG. I was leaving the farm when I saw her, just sort of staggering down the side of the road? I jumped out of the car and ran to her. Her lips were puffed up, all bloody, and it looked like somebody hauled off and hit her in the head? Mama got some wet towels to clean her off and I went right to the phone and called the Sheriff's Department. And all the whole time, Tammy kept saying, "He tried to kill me. He tried to kill me."

(Lights up on TAMMY, standing before FOUR REPORTERS –
BAND members stand as they ask their question.)

REPORTER. Are you canceling your concerts?

TAMMY. Not one. I won't give my attackers that satisfaction.

(REPORTERS raise their hands to be recognized, calling "TAMMY!".)

REPORTER ONE. Was there a Ransom Note?

(Lights up on MEEMAW and TAMMY.)

MEEMAW. No. There never was.

REPORTER TWO. Did they take your money?

MEEMAW. Not a penny. They left her car, too.

REPORTER THREE. What do you think of rumors George Jones was involved?

MEEMAW. That's downright stupid. George wouldn't do such a thing. The Police never even questioned him.

REPORTER FOUR. You've only been married to George Richey four months-

MEEMAW. *(Cuts him off.)* It wasn't him, either. Richey even took a lie detector test . Passed with flying colors.

REPORTER TWO. Do you think this is connected to the vandalism at your home?

REPORTER ONE. The break-ins?

REPORTER TWO. The fires?

REPORTER ONE. Is it true your Mother was a suspect?

MEEMAW. Me? Get out of here! No more questions! *(Reporters leave. Turns to TAMMY.)* You never answered their questions but it's time you answer mine. And I've got plenty.

TAMMY. STOP IT! You have no idea what happened! You never did. Do you think I lied about my bruises, too?

MEEMAW. I didn't say that -

TAMMY. Don't say anything! All my life you never understood a thing about me! You never even tried, you never even listened!

TAMMY'S DAUGHTER. Mom?

MEEMAW. Maybe I wasn't the only one.

TAMMY. What is it, honey?

TAMMY'S DAUGHTER. Promise you won't get all angry or upset. Because it's not just me who feels this way; all the girls do.

TAMMY. Feel what way?

TAMMY'S DAUGHTER. We're worried about you. All the pills you're taking.

TAMMY. I'm taking pain medication.

TAMMY'S DAUGHTER. Mom, you said you'd listen-

TAMMY. I've listened to you before, didn't I? I went to the Betty Ford Clinic.

TAMMY'S DAUGHTER. For three weeks-

TAMMY. Because I had emergency surgery! I was in agony! I still can't eat a real meal!

TAMMY'S DAUGHTER. Mom, let me finish-

TAMMY. I have never tried cocaine or marijuana or any kind of drug like that! Can you girls say the same? What I take is medication to help me through my shows.

TAMMY'S DAUGHTER. You can call it medication all you want; they're still drugs. And you take them now whether you're in pain or not.

TAMMY. What do you know about pain? You have no idea how I feel! You couldn't imagine it!

TAMMY'S DAUGHTER. I can't, Mom. But you can't imagine how it is seeing you sometimes. It's like you're not even here.

TAMMY. Then maybe I shouldn't be. Because I don't need accusations, I need support.

(RICHEY enters.)

RICHEY. Honey; Bill and Hilary Clinton are on 60 Minutes. You better watch this. *(He sits looking forward.)*

TAMMY'S DAUGHTER. Mom. *(TAMMY stops.)* I love you.

(TAMMY stops, hesitates.)

TAMMY. I love you, too. So, please, don't ever mention this again.

(RICHEY, TAMMY and her DAUGHTER begin watching the televisio RICHEY turns up the volume: We hear STEVE KROFT interviewing HILARY CLINTON.)

STEVE KROFT. *(V.O.)* You said your marriage has had problems. What does that mean? Does it mean adultery?

HILARY CLINTON. *(V.O.)* There isn't a person watching

who would feel comfortable sitting on their couch detailing everything that ever went on in their life and marriage. I'm not sitting here because I'm some little woman standing by my man like Tammy Wynette.

TAMMY. What did she say?

MEEMAW. *(From offstage.)* I'll kick her big butt back to Little Rock! How dare that woman!

TAMMY. *(Now just as angry.)* Why is she involving me in this thing?

(MEEMAW enters fuming.)

MEEMAW. Hilary Clinton, don't you dare talk down my daughter. Did you raise four children on your own, all the while out on the road traveling half your life? And she didn't sit back for the ride, Hilary, she drove the bus herself. Hillary, you just messed with the wrong woman's MeeMaw!

Song: *God's Gonna Get'Cha (For That)*

MEEMAW.
THIS DOGGONE WORLD WE'RE LIVING IN
IT'S GIVING ME A FIT
IT SEEMS LIKE EVERYWHERE I TURN
I SEE A HYPOCRITE
WELL IF YOU WANT TO GO TO HEAVEN
WELL YOU CAN'T LIVE LIKE THAT
SO LET ME TELL YOU SISTER
GOD'S GONNA GET'CHA FOR THAT

ALL.
GOD'S GONNA GET'CHA FOR THAT
GOD'S GONNA GET'CHA FOR THAT
THERE'S NO PLACE TO RUN AND HIDE
'CAUSE HE KNOWS WHERE YOU'RE AT
GOD'S GONNA GET'CHA FOR THAT
GOD'S GONNA GET'CHA FOR THAT
EVERY WRONG THING THAT YOU DO
GOD'S GONNA GET'CHA FOR THAT

(RICHEY has gotten the telephone.)

RICHEY. It's Hilary Clinton. She wants to apologize.
TAMMY. *(Into telephone as RICHEY holds it.)* You tell her to apologize to every Country Music Fan who's ever made it on their own with nobody taking them to the White House!
MEEMAW & DAUGHTER. *(Into telephone.)*
AMEN!

MEEMAW.
NOW THE PREACHER IN OUR CHURCH
HE'S A MIGHTY DEVOTED MAN
EVERYBODY THINKS
THAT HE'S GOING TO THE PROMISED LAND
BUT THE OTHER NIGHT ON A COUNTRY ROAD WHILE I WAS DRIVING THROUGH
I FOUND THE PREACHER MAKING LOVE
TO SISTER MARY LOU
(Overlap)

ALL EXCEPT MEEMAW.	**MEEMAW.**
GOD'S GONNA GET'CHA FOR THAT	You hear me, Hilary!
GOD'S GONNA GET'CHA FOR THAT	Don't even try to
THERE'S NO PLACE TO RUN AND HIDE	stand by your man,
FOR HE KNOWS WHERE YOU'RE AT	you'll never catch up
GOD'S GONNA GET'CHA FOR THAT	with him! That's a
GOD'S GONNA GET'CHA FOR THAT	hunting dog if I've
EVERY WRONG THING THAT YOU DO	ever seen one!
GOD'S GONNA GET'CHA FOR THAT	Forget the leash, for-
ALL	get the muzzle and
GOD'S GONNA GET'CHA FOR THAT,	go straight for the
GOD'S GONNA GET'CHA FOR THAT	hedge clippers!
THERE'S NO PLACE TO RUN AND HIDE	
FOR HE KNOWS WHERE YOU'RE AT	
GOD'S GONNA GET'CHA FOR THAT	
GOD'S GONNA GET'CHA FOR THAT	
EVERY WRONG THING THAT YOU DO	
GOD'S GONNA GET'CHA FOR THAT	
EVERY WRONG THING THAT YOU DO	

GOD'S GONNA GET'CHA FOR THAT

(Lights fade, then restore to indicate passage of time.)

TAMMY, "Mu Mu Land"? Why in the world would you give me this song? I can't even tell what it's supposed to be. Funk? Rap?

RICHEY. It's Pop.

TAMMY. This song couldn't go pop with a mouth full of fire-crackers. Why would Kentucky Fried Chicken even write such a thing?

RICHEY. It's the KLF, not KFC. It's a change for you, sure, but what's wrong with that? You've got nothing to lose and every-thing to gain. They want to record here and film the video in London with some hot MTV director.

TAMMY. Read these lyrics.

RICHEY. Read them?

TAMMY. That's right. Read them and tell me what they mean.

RICHEY. *(Reading)*
"ALL BOUND FOR MUMULAND
ALL BOUND FOR MUMULAND
HEY
HEY HEY
ALL BOUND FOR MUMUMULAND"

TAMMY. And where is MuMuland, exactly?

RICHEY. Maybe it explains later on if you read it-

TAMMY. No, no, Richey. You keep reading.

RICHEY.
"THEY'RE JUSTIFIED AND THEY'RE ANCIENT
AND THEY DRIVE AN ICE CREAM VAN
THEY'RE JUSTIFIED AND THEY'RE ANCIENT
I HOPE YOU'LL UNDERSTAND"

TAMMY. You're right! It all makes sense now!

RICHEY. Tammy-

TAMMY. No, Richey. I'd rather sing the phone book. Say goodbye to MuMuland.

RICHEY. All right, then. Clive Davis just thought it would expand your audience. I reckon I can explain it to the grandkids.

    TAMMY. What do they have to do with this?

    RICHEY. They think the KLF is "cool". They think this song is "cool". And they think you'd be "really cool" if you sang it. Tammy; how bad can it be?

(TAMMY stares at RICHEY; He smiles. "Justified and Ancient" begins playing.)

A Sound Stage

(The DIRECTOR of the video wears a yellow hood over his head and carries a video camera. He films close ups of TAMMY. Company will enter during chorus)

Song: *Justified And Ancient (Mumu Land)*

ALL.
ALL BOUND FOR MUMU LAND
ALL BOUND FOR MUMU LAND
HEY, HEY— ALL BOUND FOR MUMU LAND
HEY, HEY— ALL BOUND FOR MUMU LAND

TAMMY.
THEY'RE JUSTIFIED AND THEY'RE ANCIENT
AND THEY LIKE TO ROAM THE LAND
THEY'RE JUSTIFIED AND THEY'RE ANCIENT
AND THEY DRIVE AND ICE CREAM VAN

THEY CALLED ME UP IN TENNESSEE
THEY SAID "TAMMY, STAND BY THE JAM"
BUT IF YOU DON'T LIKE WHAT THEY'RE GOING TO DO
BETTER NOT STOP THEM 'CAUSE THEY'RE COMING THROUGH

ALL.
HEY HEY
ALL BOUND FOR MUMULAND
HEY HEY

ALL BOUND FOR MUMULAND
MUMULAND, MUMULAND
ALL BOUND FOR MUMULAND—HEY!

MEEMAW. If I wasn't dead already, that woulda killed me.

*(Lights blackout - Musical playout - TAMMY gets into hospital
    bed.)*

HEY HEY ALL BOUND FOR MUMULAND
HEY HEY ALL BOUND FOR MUMULAND

<u>A Hospital Room</u>

(TAMMY is in pain; tries to hide it.)

BILLY. No hospitals in MuMuland? Five days in a coma; that
song only put me out for one. Now it's a hit in eighteen countries, I
should check myself in here. How are you?
    TAMMY. *(Weak, but smiling.)* Better. They had to do an intes-
tinal by-pass and then the scar tissue got infected.
    BILLY. So you'd better start writing. You and Jones are the
only two people I know who can turn catastrophe into a hit single.
I can hear it now "Stand By Your Scar Tissue".
    TAMMY. *(Laughs)* Well, if it keeps me working.
    BILLY. I'm getting out.
    TAMMY. *(Stunned)* What?
    BILLY. I'm getting out of the business.
    TAMMY. Billy, you are the business.
    BILLY. You always said this town was like some Boy's Club,
and you weren't all wrong. But things are changing. It might still be
a Boy's Club, but it's going to be run by Boys who think talent
means putting a pretty girl in her tightest jeans. Just listen to the
Radio. No matter what station I turn on, I never hear you or George,
not even Patsy or Hank. Legends. All of you. And legends are born,
not made. I made great country music, and I don't give a damn
about great album covers. *(Pause)* I never talked this much in my
life.
    TAMMY. What will you do?

BILLY. Strap my guitar to the tallest mast on my boat and sail south. And I'm not going to stop 'till I tie up to the first port where somebody points up to my guitar and says, "What the hell is that?"

(Light's fade as BILLY exits, TAMMY exits. Lights up on RICHEY pursued by TAMMY'S DAUGHTER.)

<u>Backstage Before A Concert</u>

TAMMY'S DAUGHTER. Richey, mom's so tired I can't even wake her up.

RICHEY. She'll be fine.

TAMMY'S DAUGHTER. She's not "fine". She's sick. I'm calling a hospital.

RICHEY. Don't.

TAMMY'S DAUGHTER. Why not?

RICHEY. Sweetie, you mother wouldn't want that.

TAMMY'S DAUGHTER. How do you have any idea what my mother wants? She's been stretched out in her dressing room all day! She can't make it to the stage, let alone through a show! She'll collapse out there!

RICHEY. You know there's nothing I wouldn't do for Tammy.

TAMMY'S DAUGHHTER. Then cancel the show!

RICHEY. You tell your Mother that. She rests up for weeks just to step on stage. And while you're at it, tell the band they're not getting paychecks, either.

TAMMY'S DAUGHTER. Is that what it comes down to? Paychecks? Richey, this will kill her!

(TAMMY talks quietly, short of breath.)

TAMMY. No, honey. This keeps me alive.

TAMMY'S DAUGHTER. Mom-

TAMMY. *(Holds her arm for support.)* Just stand with me a second.

(Music begins.)

GEORGE RICHEY. *(Hearing TAMMY'S cue.)* Ready?

TAMMY. Ready.

<u>A Concert</u>

(TAMMY makes her way slowly toward a stool sitting center stage. As TAMMY hears the applause and feels the heat of the lights, she seems to walk taller, gaining strength from it. TAMMY waves, smiling now, sitting on the stool.)

TAMMY. I'd like to do a song tonight I haven't done for awhile. I wrote it years ago for my girls, Gwen, Jackie, Tina, Georgette, Kelly and Deirdre who now have little boys and girls of their own. Maybe times have changed, but what I feel for them never has. *(Turns to band.)* Boys; "Dear Daughters"

Song: *Dear Daughters*

TAMMY.
DEAR GWEN, YOU'RE MY OLDEST. YOU'RE QUITE A LADY
MY ONLY BLUE EYED GIRL
YOU TURNED SIXTEEN IN APRIL AND
YOU SURE MADE A CHANGE IN MY WORLD.
I'M SORRY I MISSED THE BIG EVENING, YOUR FIRST DATE
AND I WASN'T AROUND
SAVE ALL THE SECRET THINGS YOU DID
AND TELL ME WHEN I GET TO TOWN
AND ON YOUR GRADUATION, I WANTED PICTURES TO LOOK BACK ON
BUT I WASN'T THERE TO TAKE THEM.
AS USUAL I WAS GONE.

YOU'VE HAD TO GROW UP MUCH TOO QUICK,
AND YOU'VE DONE IT ON YOUR OWN
YOU DID IT WITHOUT MAMA
BECAUSE MAMA WASN'T HOME

AND JACKIE,
YOU'RE QUITE A LADY, TOO

YOU'RE JUST ONE YEAR YOUNGER THAN GWEN
AND THERE'S SO MUCH THAT I'M MISSING
BY BEING MOMMY NOW AND THEN.
I REMEMBER THE DAY YOU COOKED YOUR FIRST MEAL
YOU WERE JUST NINE; YOU COOKED BISCUITS AND
HAM.
YOU CALLED TO ME HOW GOOD IT WAS
'CAUSE I WAS OUT OF TOWN

AND THE PARTY FOR
FATHERS AND DAUGHTERS
I KNOW YOU FELT OUT OF PLACE
EVEN THE PRETTY DRESS I BOUGHT
COULDN'T FILL THAT EMPTY SPACE
AND THE TIME WHEN YOU GOT SICK
AND THE DOCTOR TURNED YOU DOWN
THEY SAID THEY COULDN'T TREAT YOU
WITH YOUR MAMA OUT OF TOWN

AND TINA,
YOU'RE SUCH A PRETTY GIRL
WITH BIG ALMOND EYES OF BROWN
THEY VOTED YOU HOMECOMING QUEEN
WHILE I WAS OUT OF TOWN
I KNOW YOU WERE A BEAUTY
'CAUSE YOUR SISTERS DRESSED YOU RIGHT
AND YOU SAID IT DIDN'T MATTER
THAT I COULDN'T BE THERE THAT NIGHT

AND THE DAY YOU JOINED THE CHEERING TEAM
NOTHING COULD HOLD YOU DOWN
YOU YELLED "HIP HIP HOORAY" OVER THE PHONE
'CAUSE AS USUAL
I WAS OUT OF TOWN

AND TAMALA GEORGETTE JONES
YOU SIMPLY TAKE MY BREATH AWAY
BORN JUST SIX SHORT YEARS AGO
AND NAMED FOR YOUR DADDY AND ME

GOING TO SLEEP ON MEEMAW'S ARM
LISTENING TO HER HUM
DRIFTING OFF TO FAIRYLAND
WHILE SUCKING ON YOUR THUMB

JUST YESTERDAY YOU PULLED A TOOTH
BOY, YOU SURE ARE BRAVE AND STRONG
I WISH I COULD HAVE BEEN THERE
BUT AS USUAL
I WAS GONE

(Music changes: Singing My Song.)

    TAMMY. Thank you so much. It's because of all of you that I'm up here, singing my song.

Song: *Singing My Song*

    TAMMY.
HERE'S A SONG I LOVE TO SING
IT'S ABOUT THE MAN THAT WEARS MY RING
AND EVEN THO' HE'S TEMPTED, HE KNOWS
I'LL MAKE SURE THAT HE GETS EV'RYTHING
CAUSE WHEN HE'S COLD HE KNOWS I'M WARM
AND I WANT HIM IN MY ARMS
AND WHEN HE'S SAD, OH, I MAKE HIM GLAD
AND I'M HIS SHELTER FROM THE STORM

I'M HIS SONG WHEN HE FEELS LIKE SINGIN'
AND I SWING WHEN HE FEELS LIKE SWINGIN'
I DON'T KNOW WHAT I DO THAT'S RIGHT
BUT IT MAKES HIM COME HOME AT NIGHT
AND WHEN HE'S HOME
I MAKE SURE HE'S NEVER ALONE
AND THAT'S WHY I KEEP SINGIN' MY SONG

AND WHEN HE'S HOME
I MAKE SURE HE'S NEVER ALONE
AND THAT'S WHY I KEEP SINGIN' MY SONG,
MY SONG!

(Blackout)

<u>Tammy And Richey's Home In Nashville</u>

(TAMMY is stretched out on their couch. As TAMMY and her DAUGHTER speak, GEORGE RICHEY enters, putting an IV in place.)

TAMMY'S DAUGHTER. Dolly called while you were asleep. She told me to congratulate the only singer at the Rain Forest Benefit to get a standing ovation. *(Sits on couch.)* Are these the pictures? *(Looks at them.)*

TAMMY. We drove the bus up to New York City. So there we were parked outside Carnegie Hall cooking pinto beans and corn bread.

TAMMY'S DAUGHTER. Mom! You didn't tell me all these people were there!

RICHEY. You should have been backstage. Everybody was lining up for your mother's autograph. Pavarotti, Whitney Houston, James Taylor.

TAMMY'S DAUGHTER. That's you and Sting!

TAMMY. I was so disappointed all he wanted was an autograph.

(They laugh.)

TAMMY'S DAUGHTER. I'd better go and pick up the kids. See you later.

TAMMY. Give them a kiss for me. *(TAMMY'S DAUGHTER stops for a momen.)* Forget something?

TAMMY'S DAUGHTER. Yes I did.

(Goes back and kisses TAMMY.)

TAMMY. Bye.
TAMMY'S DAUGHTER. Bye.

(TAMMY'S DAUGHTER leaves.)

RICHEY. Are you hungry?

TAMMY. Not much.

RICHEY. Something to drink? Ice tea? Water?

TAMMY. I've got some water. *(RICHEY and TAMMY finish administering IV.)* I'm just going to take a nap.

RICHEY. You read my mind.

(RICHEY lays down next to her. TAMMY'S former husbands begin to assemble around the stage.)

TAMMY. When Jackie's girls were here last week, I taught them to sing "How Great Thou Art"; I sang it in church when I was their age. I showed them pictures in the Bible of Jesus as a Little Boy and told them how he was God's Only Son. That did it. Both the twins looked up at me and Catherine said, "Grandma, doesn't God have any daughters?" *(TAMMY smiles; LIGHTS slowly start to change.)* Richey; are you asleep?

RICHEY. Yes.

TAMMY. Sometimes I can't tell whether I am or not.

(Through the scrim upstage we see YOUNG TAMMY, she sings as RICHEY and TAMMY fall asleep.)

Song: How Great Thou Art

YOUNG TAMMY.
THEN SINGS MY SOUL MY SAVIOR GOD TO THEE
HOW GREAT THOU ART HOW GREAT THOU ART

(MEEMAW enters.)

THEN SINGS MY SOUL MY SAVIOR GOD TO THEE
HOW GREAT THOU ART, HOW GREAT THOU ART

(MEEMAW gently wakes TAMMY.)

TAMMY.
Mee Maw! Where have you been?

MEEMAW. It's 1998. I've been dead five years. Can't an old woman get rest around here?

TAMMY.

I know what you want me to say now: I was addicted. But it wasn't what you think. Looking back like this, I see how much my life changed. But I never changed with it. I was always that little girl singing on my Daddy's lap when he plays the guitar. You say I didn't know him, but I know one thing: he loved me. And I felt the same way every time I stepped out on a stage, seeing all those people. I don't know them, either, but I can see in their faces, smiling, crying; they wanted me to sing. They never left me. They were my addiction. Everything else, that was to stop the pain in between.

MEEMAW. *(Hard to get out.)* Your Daddy, he loved to sing-

TAMMY. I know.

MEEMAW. No. You don't. He wanted to be a singer. A real singer, just like you.

TAMMY. MeeMaw; why didn't you tell me?

MEEMAW. Tell you what? That he had a wife who said "No"? A wife afraid he'd fail? Afraid he'd leave her? Then he got sick and did, all the same. *(Pause; composes herself.)* They're calling you an "Artist". Well, I don't know anything about "Art". But sometimes I see a picture on some wall and I say, 'That's right. That's just the way it looks. I can just feel that breeze and smell the wheat on the field'. Those people out there, they say the same thing when you sing. 'That's right. That's the way I feel, too. I'm not alone. And you become something bigger, something bigger than you are all by yourself. If that's being an Artist, it's something to be proud of. What I'm trying to say is that I'm proud, too. My daughter is Tammy Wynette. You took care of your family. Now it's time you let your family take care of you. Don't be afraid.

(TAMMY gets up from the bed, looks at RICHEY; A guitar continues to play softly.)

TAMMY. MeeMaw, do you hear that?

MEEMAW. Go on. See for yourself. Sounds to me like somebody's Daddy playing the guitar.

(Lights up on MAN in shadows up center. He begins to play "Stand By Your Man" on a guitar. TAMMY faces upstage and begins to sing; at first, her voice is faltering before it builds. As

TAMMY starts to sing, her husband who have assembled around her, slowly begin to cross by her. They return to their positions in the band, with the music growing as each gets into place.)

Song: *Stand By Your Man*

TAMMY.
SOMETIMES IT'S HARD TO BE A WOMAN
GIVIN' ALL YOUR LOVE TO JUST ONE MAN
YOU'LL HAVE BAD TIMES
AND HE'LL HAVE GOOD TIMES
DOIN' THINGS THAT YOU DON'T UNDERSTAND

BUT IF YOU LOVE HIM YOU'LL FORGIVE HIM
EVEN THOUGH HE'S HARD TO UNDERSTAND
AND IF YOU LOVE HIM
OH, BE PROUD OF HIM
'CAUSE, AFTER ALL, HE'S JUST A MAN

STAND BY YOUR MAN
GIVE HIM TWO ARMS TO CLING TO
AND SOMETHING WARM TO COME TO
WHEN NIGHTS ARE COLD AND LONELY
STAND BY YOUR MAN
AND SHOW THE WORLD YOU LOVE HIM
KEEP GIVIN' ALL THE LOVE YOU CAN
STAND BY YOUR MAN

STAND BY YOUR MAN
AND SHOW THE WORLD YOU LOVE HIM
KEEP GIVIN' ALL THE LOVE YOU CAN
STAND BY YOUR MAN

(TAMMY turns, runs into her father's arms upstage.)

(BLACKOUT)

THE END

www.ingramcontent.com/pod-product-compliance
Lightning Source LLC
Chambersburg PA
CBHW070352120726
47909CB00008B/2818